VERTICAL WORLD ∀

THE WRECKAGE OF THE PAST

BY BRIAN CRAWFORD

EPIC Escape

An Imprint of EPIC Press
abdopublishing.com

The Wreckage of the Past
Vertical World: Book #5

abdopublishing.com

Published by EPIC Press, a division of ABDO, PO Box 398166, Minneapolis, Minnesota 55439. Copyright © 2019 by Abdo Consulting Group, Inc. International copyrights reserved in all countries. No part of this book may be reproduced in any form without written permission from the publisher. Escape™ is a trademark and logo of EPIC Press.

Printed in the United States of America, North Mankato, Minnesota.
052018
092018

Cover design by Christina Doffing
Images for cover art obtained from iStockphoto.com
Edited by Gil Conrad

Library of Congress Cataloging-in-Publication Data

Library of Congress Control Number: 2018932905

Publisher's Cataloging in Publication Data

Names: Crawford, Brian, author.
Title: The wreckage of the past/ by Brian Crawford
Description: Minneapolis, MN : EPIC Press, 2019 | Series: Vertical world; #5
Summary: Having escaped Ætheria, Aral and Rex take refuge on Cthonia near the impact site of Ætheria's power plant. At the same time, a team of armed Cthonian scouts sets out to recover their dead from the destruction. Among them, the Ætherian refugee Máire Himmel offers her knowledge of Ætheria to identify remnants of the destroyed power plant.
Identifiers: ISBN 9781680769159 (lib. bdg.) | ISBN 9781680769432 (ebook)
Subjects: LCSH: Teenage refugees--Fiction. | Survival--Fiction--Fiction. | Revolutions--Fiction--Fiction. | Science fiction--Societies, etc--Fiction | Young adult fiction.
Classification: DDC [FIC]--dc23

T 27189

This series is dedicated to Debbie Pearson.
Thank you for everything.

ONE

WHEN ARAL PRIED OPEN REX'S DESCENT pod, his body tumbled out headfirst.

The sudden weight of his limp torso almost made her fall the ten feet backward to the Cthonian sand. Because his pod had come down from Ætheria after Aral's, it had come to rest on top of hers, like the second bead in a giant necklace stretching up into the toxic Welcans cloud. Aral's pod had touched down smoothly, but Rex hadn't come out of his. After waiting several minutes, Aral had decided something was wrong and scrambled up her pod to his.

"Ugh!" she groaned as Rex fell forward. She was able to stop his fall with her right shoulder, but she could not let go of the pod's hatch frame with her left hand. As soon as his stomach folded over her, she wrapped her right arm around him and squeezed. His body was made even more awkward by a bulky yet tightly wound sling that held his right arm across his stomach.

Seeing the sling again, Aral felt a warmth of emotion. He'd injured himself to get to her. Without the injury, he never would've been able to reach her in her torture room. And if he hadn't come, the two wouldn't have escaped. But surely there was something she didn't know. Why had that Protector, Challies, helped them? What was he going to get out of it? Would he be punished?

Clutching the edge of the pod's door, Aral glanced into Rex's pod, which glowed softly from fading control lights. What she saw made her jump.

On the left side of the compartment where Rex had stood during the descent, a yard-long burn mark ran the length of where his torso had been. It looked as if someone had taken a large piece of black chalk or charcoal and drawn a rough line from the hip to the shoulder. At each end, the line ended in a splash of black, as ash spread out like a star.

No sooner had Aral registered the large smudge than the acrid smell of burning cloth stung her nose. Feeling Rex's dead weight on her shoulder, she realized: Rex's pod had been struck by lightning on the way down.

Heart racing, she clambered to the ground. Rex's arm and legs dangled as she moved. Though she was much taller than he, Aral felt her thighs burn with the effort of laying him down faceup. When his head came to rest, it lay at an upward angle, as if he were trying to point to the sky with his chin or dig into the ground with the back of his head. Aral remained on her knees at his side. Her face hovered a foot above his.

Aral examined his features. She'd known him for just less than a week, but she continued to be amazed by the darkness of his skin. She couldn't imagine spending her life—as he did—so close to the sun. It was a wonder to her how anyone survived in Ætheria. Now, Aral saw nothing different in his complexion. His mouth was slightly open, as were his eyes, revealing thin slits of white at the bottoms of his eyelids.

"Rex!" she said at almost a shout.

Hearing her own voice made her start. She raised her upper body and looked around, expecting to be overheard. There was no one in sight. All she saw was the same bland Cthonian desert. The air glowed yellow, lit by the diffuse moonlight trying in vain to penetrate the clouds above. The rain from several days before had left no trace. The ground was bone-dry, and the air swirled with wafts of stinging dust. Only the hundreds of guy wires and support poles marred the landscape.

"Rex!" Aral shouted. She placed her hand on his uninjured shoulder and leaned forward. She turned her head to the side and eased her ear close to Rex's mouth and nose. A soft hiss escaped his lips. He was breathing.

A mixture of relief and fear flooded Aral—relief that he was alive, but fear because he was not waking up. When she was training for her search assignments on the eqūs, she'd never been shown what to do in case of another's injury. She placed her left hand on Rex's other shoulder and squeezed with both hands. Maybe by squeezing his injured shoulder as well, she thought, she could cause him just enough pain to wake up.

No reaction.

She squeezed again, this time harder. Rex groaned and rolled his head to the side.

"Rex?"

He mumbled a response. She squeezed even harder, making sure to pinch his wounded shoulder. He winced.

"Rex? It's Aral. Can you hear me?"

He opened his eyes and blinked. He seemed to be trying to focus an eye that wasn't responding. He blinked again and turned his head to face her. She hovered over his face. His pupils were dilated and distant. Glassy. He seemed to be looking straight through her.

"Aral?" he whispered. "Mom? Is that you? Mom?"

"No, it's Aral. From below . . . from Cthonia. But I *do* know your mom. Remember? You showed me her picture. She told me about you . . . your name . . . about your face . . . She told everyone . . . Let's go find her."

"Whaaaaa . . . ?"

"Can you sit up?"

Aral released his shoulders and slid her left arm under his shoulder blades. She tensed her muscles and lifted slowly, gently, urging him up. He blinked and reached out with his good left arm. With her free hand, Aral took his arm and placed it on the ground. The sand scratching into his palm, he pushed up and sat. Once he was fully seated, he shook the sand from his hand and rubbed his eyes like someone with a vicious headache. His hair was tousled and messy, as if he were just waking up from sleeping fourteen hours.

"What happened? Ugh . . . "

"Your pod was hit by lightning. As we were coming down. It must've knocked you out. But at least it didn't do any more harm . . . at least as far as I can tell. You're lucky to be alive."

"Coming down? What?" He shook his head, confused.

"You . . . you and Challies . . . the Protector from Ætheria. Both of you helped me get out of that building, that room. Up there." She pointed. "In Ætheria." Even though Rex wasn't looking at her, she nodded skywards. "They were torturing me. Cutting off my oxygen. You came and got me out, and we escaped. We took the pods to get back down. They were chasing us. Shooting at us. I almost froze to death. Do you remember?"

Rex slowly began to nod. He opened his eyes and

looked around, squinting like someone staring into the sun.

"Yes . . . I remember. What's going on? What are we going to do? Mom . . . " He brought his free hand to his head and massaged his temples.

"Listen. Right now, we need to move. We don't have any choice. Get away from here." Aral looked up. Only the dark expanse of the nighttime desert met her gaze. She gaped at the faint shadows of hundreds of guy wires and support struts extending thousands of feet upward before disappearing into the clouds above. Seeing the poles now, she marveled at how no one on Cthonia really knew what stood atop these poles . . . some people may have had an inkling from what Máire had told them, sure, but all they could imagine was some oppressive tribal group of people—*skiélodytes*, as some Cthonians called them. Of the all the Cthonians, Aral realized right then that she was the only one who *really* knew what Ætheria was like. But when she'd been up there, she'd only seen it from the inside of buildings, as a prisoner. What did it look like on the outside? What did the direct sun look like? Feel like? Did it burn your skin?

"Can you stand up?" she asked, shaking away her thoughts. "Are you hurt?"

"My shoulder's killing me. That's all, really. I think. And I have a headache . . . right here." He pointed to his forehead. "But nothing else, I think. Here." He extended his good arm. Aral stood and gripped his forearm, pulling him up gently but firmly. Working together, they eased him up, but he leaned on her for support. Because she was nearly a foot taller than he, his head fell just below her shoulder. She placed her arm around him and wedged her hand under his armpit. She squeezed gently, offering support. He grimaced at the pressure.

"Come on, let's go," she said, taking a small step westward. "You can do it. It's still early morning, so we have time. But we've got to move."

Rex nodded.

"Where?"

Aral looked up and squinted at the western horizon.

"From here we need to get to where your building came down . . . where our group was set up. I doubt things are still burning from the explosion. From here I can't see much. It's too dark. Let's at least get to the impact site now. Do you remember? There, there's an airship. One of ours. If we can get there, we'll at least have shelter. Of course," she paused, "that is, hoping that the Cthonians that shot at us aren't still hanging around and waiting for us. But I would be surprised.

"When we get there, you can rest and I can try to find some supplies to help us make it the rest of the way. When you all found me before, I'd just come across our water and food lockers. They hadn't been damaged. If they're still there, then we might make it. If not, well, I don't know if we'll get all the way . . ."

"All the way where?"

"To the Cthonian Cave Complex."

"But . . . we were *shot* at. If they are still there, won't they just shoot again?"

Aral took a deep breath. "Yeah, they did shoot at us. And no, I don't know if they're still there. How could I? But that was a few days ago now. Maybe they are. But," she paused, reflecting, "they also shot at us because you shot at them first. Remember? They probably thought . . . "

"Oh, yeah, you're right. But that was an accident! My gun was broken, I . . . "

"I know, I know. *I* believe you. Maybe they couldn't see your face. Who knows? They were high up. Those lights were so bright . . . " She paused, wondering if the Cthonians had recognized her as well.

"But still," she continued. "I don't see what other option we have. This is a desert. The rain's acidic. We stay here and we'll die for sure. We can't go back up; they're after us." She looked up. "And I'd bet they're on their way down after us. So we need to go. Here, yes, maybe they are looking for me, I don't know. The only thing I can think of is that we surrender to those Cthonians who were after us, assuming they're at the impact site. Because I'm also sure that I know your mother, or at least know *about* her. I haven't spoken to her in years. She's been here since when I was born, and *everyone* in the CCC has heard of her. I don't know, but I think that the only way we're going to be able to get anywhere is by getting you to her. If we can surrender and get back to the Cthonian Cave Complex, we can show them who you are, get you two together, and then . . . "

"And then what?" Rex's heart surged at the thought that he was getting close to his mother, whose face he'd seen only in a photograph.

"And then we'll see."

Images of his mother swirled through Rex's pounding brain. These were versions of the picture he'd found in his foster dad's bedroom cabinet. But Rex *had* found it.

Discovering the picture had triggered an

onslaught of buried emotions—emotions he'd never known he'd had. His mom, who his foster dad had always said had just left when Rex was a baby. But why, he'd never said. Rex could only guess. At her mention now, though, Rex was too overcome with pain from his shoulder and head to feel anything else. He felt numb to emotions. He felt numb to Aral's plan. He felt numb to everything that was happening between Ætheria and Cthonia.

Right now, all he wanted to do was lie down and rest.

TWO

"THIS JUST IN FROM THE FRONT: TENSIONS *are mounting as a Cthonian air brigade gave hot pursuit to a band of infiltrators from above the clouds.*

"Here is what we know so far:

"A Cthonian airship had scrambled to the scene in response to the catastrophic collapse of some sort of structure that fell from above the clouds, horrifically killing forty Cthonian operatives sent as water seekers and emissaries to the Ætherians. Not three miles from the disaster site, the team encountered a group of forces that seemed to have been sent from Ætheria. Though

they were flying at an altitude of three hundred feet, the team recognized the Ætherians by what Cthonian officials are now describing as an exceedingly short stature, dark skin, and barrel-like torsos.

"The air brigade's first response was, according to standard operating procedure, to land the airship and engage the combatants peacefully.

"Unfortunately for mounting tensions between our two worlds, the infiltrators fired upon the Cthonian airship, triggering the appropriate response from our heroic Cthonian spotters.

"Upon successfully engaging and neutralizing most of the enemy, our air brigade gave pursuit. But two Ætherians disappeared into Ætheria's network of support guy wires and metal struts. Not expecting this unprovoked attack and ill-equipped for a hostile encounter, the airship was immediately ordered back to the Cthonian Cave Complex. And as we speak, armaments and reinforcements are being prepared for a second sortie, this time with the goal of securing the impact site and conducting a full investigation. Because *of the airships' age, they won't be ready for flight for another few days. When we know . . . "*

Click.

Máire Himmel slammed her hand on the broadcasting receiver, silencing it. Her heart pounded. She wrung her hands as she processed the news. *It's too early for this,* she thought, rolling over in bed and glancing at her glowing alarm clock. Almost 06:00. She turned onto her back and stared at her ceiling, which was bathed in morning black.

She stifled a *humph* in the dark and shook her head. Ætheria and Cthonia had come into contact . . . *violent* contact. Not since she came down from Ætheria sixteen years before had she thought much about the tyranny of the Ætherian leadership. Her son, yes; she thought about him every day. Was he still alive? Had he been able to get beyond his birth handicap? Was he normal? But whether or not Cthonia and Ætheria could cooperate? There was no need to think about it. The two worlds kept to themselves like two tribes separated by miles of dense rain forest. Only now—now that Cthonia's underground water source had dried up—did the Cthonians have any need to reach out to the Ætherians for help. But what had the Ætherians done?

Attack, that's what.

She was sure the Head Ductor was behind the conflict—it was he, after all, who had any undesirables in Ætheria murdered by being Tossed from the islands above to fall to their deaths. It was he who prevented regular Ætherians from having oxygen, without which most of the population lived in a perpetual state of hypoxia.

Eyes wide open, Máire could only guess at the tight forms of her sleeping tube. Measuring seven feet long and with a diameter of three feet, the tubes provided enough privacy for sleep, yet allowed Cthonia to make the most of what little space they had underground. When pollution had reached dangerous levels nearly a millennium ago and rain had become more and more acidic, humans had sought refuge in whatever caves they could find. Cthonia had succeeded in colonizing a massive cave. Although the cave held nearly two thousand people in tight quarters, it left little room for large apartments or personal space. Only command officials were allowed actual rooms for themselves. Everyone else was assigned a personal sleeping tube with a shade that could be pulled for privacy, a shared bathroom, and shared food preparation facilities. Everything was shared in Cthonia, especially the crops of harvested, underground fungus that the Cthonians had learned to cultivate and digest.

Even though it was still too early to get up, Máire's mind raced too much to let her fall back asleep. Ever since the news had been reported that Cthonia's forces had found the Ætherian supports and water extraction tube, too many memories had flooded her . . . memories and fears. *Would they come for her? Did they even know she was here?*

"No," she said aloud, squinting away the thoughts. She knew far too much about what life was really like in Ætheria . . . even though it all had been sixteen years ago. *Maybe they thought she was dead? Maybe they'd just assumed she'd never made it down through the poisonous Welcans cloud when she was forced to leave . . . ?*

Her thoughts gathered speed once more. Cursing under her breath, she pushed up her sleeping tube shade with her bare feet and slid out. Like an agile spider, she worked her way out of her tube and scrambled to the cold stone floor.

Walking on the balls of her feet, she hurried down to the communal bathroom at the end of the dormitory corridor. She stepped in and flicked on the light. It hummed its fluorescent glare into her eyes, making her squint. She stepped up to the mirror and rubbed her face with her hands. Moving instinctively, she reached down and turned the washbasin faucet. A low hiss of air emerged. She shook her head, remembering that Cthonia's water supply had been cut . . . that's why they were now facing the belligerent Ætherians, after all. She looked in the mirror and stared at her reflection.

Despite her forty-nine years, the person gazing back at her seemed more than seventy. Worry lines radiated from the corners of her eyes. Dark bags on her upper cheeks betrayed her lack of restful sleep over the past few days. Her eyes were bloodshot, but her pupils and irises glowed with an intense intelligence.

Before, in her former life, she'd grown accustomed to looking at everyone except her newborn son Rex with suspicion. Looking over her shoulder, expecting to be overwhelmed, taken prisoner . . . these had become her way of life. When she'd finally escaped and made it to Cthonia, only then could she begin to relax. Yes, she was different than the other Cthonians. Yes, they had at first eyed her warily, but at the same time there had been a certain curiosity. She was a marvel, an asylum-seeker from *up there* who'd decided to give up savage ways of life to come to true civilization . . . to Cthonia.

More than that, when she'd first arrived *down below*, much of her former worry had been erased by the incredible new strength that Cthonia's denser air had provided her lungs and her body. Seeing how she felt now—how she could run, how she rarely felt tired—she couldn't imagine going back to a vertical world of hypoxia. *How could they be so stupid?* She'd often thought about the Ætherians, and especially the Head Ductor and all his growing paranoia about oxygen. *Didn't they know they were killing themselves by staying up there so long? That they were starving their brains of oxygen? Why were they being so stubborn?*

She rubbed her eyes once more and blinked at her reflection. There, the darkened face of an Ætherian stared back at her. Because she was much shorter than the Cthonians, her head was framed in the lower portion of the mirror. She blinked again and wondered at how her skin had maintained its darkness despite her sixteen years in the sun-deprived, cloudy world below.

She also wondered if her son Rex, whom she'd last seen when he was only two weeks old, might look anything like her . . . now that he was sixteen and becoming a man.

If he was alive.

THREE

DESPITE THE INSULATION HIS REGULATION ACF AeroGel suit provided, the subzero temperature in Island Twenty-Two's Larder was beginning to get to Protector Challies. He'd been hidden under the island's surface for only an hour, maybe two, but Challies quickly realized he would need to get out of there, and soon.

For one thing, he had counted on the Larder being able to keep him alive for days, weeks even. After all, all members of the ACF knew these hidden, subterranean storerooms held emergency supplies for all of Ætheria: water, food, AG suits, battery-powered lanterns, rappelling harnesses, winches, climbing gloves, carabiners, survival kits, and spare SCRMs . . . but without the oxygen canisters to connect them to. *So what's the point?* Challies thought as he rummaged around his hide's supplies. For another, the Larder's water reserves were frozen and the entire room was frigid. When he discovered this, Challies instantly recalled that when Ætheria's Power Works had been attacked, the heating throughout the archipelago had been cut. This included the Larders. The only places still heated were the Sanatorium, Bernuac HQ, the community centers, and Ætheria's Council Complex—where the members of the Ætherian Council worked.

Without heat, the Larders—and every other building in Ætheria—were little more than massive freezers. *Why hadn't I thought of that before?* he cursed himself. He knew his AG suit could only stave off hypothermia for sixteen hours. Or at least according to the suit's "official specifications." If he didn't do something, he'd die in here . . . just like the three Cthonian spies that had been found nearly two weeks before. He swore at himself. He should've found somewhere else to hide from the ACF after helping Rex and Aral.

But it was too late. He was here, and now he had to do something.

But what?

Challies knew that getting caught would mean getting Tossed. Since the escape had just happened, he assumed that all of Ætheria—Island Twenty-Two especially—was crawling with ACF determined to find him, Rex, and Aral. *Had Rex and Aral even made it out?* he wondered. Going back up top was not an option—at least not for now.

That left only one choice: going down.

Besides being storerooms for emergency supplies, most Larders contained downward-facing hatches. These allowed maintenance crews access to the guy wires stabilizing the Ætherian islands against the powerful stratospheric winds. At the center of each Larder, what looked like a metal pole stretched from floor to ceiling, where it was attached by a series of massive bolts. But this was not a pole. It was a woven steel wire as thick as an adult's arm.

While one end was bolted to the ceiling, the other disappeared through two trap doors in the floor. From there, the wire stretched downward for twenty feet before separating into eight thinner wires spreading out and down. Wider and wider they extended, until they reached Cthonia thirty thousand feet below, where they were secured to ten-ton stone anchors buried twenty feet into the ground. These, along with a network of thirty to fifty rigid stratoneum struts per island, were the only thing keeping Ætheria from plummeting six miles to the Cthonian wasteland. The wires could not fail. They had to be diligently and regularly maintained. And to do this, teams of ACF scouts would attach harnesses and rappel down, using a mechanized winch to climb back up. In this way, they could inspect every inch of the wires once a month.

During his time in the ACF, Challies had never been part of the maintenance teams.

But now he wished he had.

From within the Larder, it was difficult to hear much of what was happening outside. With the wind howling below, and the thick hatch cover above, Challies felt as if he were in a soundproof room. Were the ACF right on top of him? Had more been called to the island since Rex and Aral's escape? Why hadn't anyone checked the Larder? The only thing Challies could think of was that Bernuac HQ had seen that Challies's Nanokepp Card had been used to cross the Zipp lines—not Rex's. Because Challies had given his card to Rex, the ACF probably thought that he too had escaped below.

Or so he hoped.

Using one of the battery-powered lanterns stocked in the Larder's shelves, Challies squatted in the center of the room, eyeing the trap door carefully. The piercing white light danced off the wire's shiny woven metal, projecting a dazzling constellation around the otherwise black room.

Seeing no latch, lever, or button on the trap door itself or around its frame, Challies reached out and ran his fingers along the flaps' joint. The device was clearly made out of stratoneum—the ultralight yet impregnable metal that formed the skeleton of most of Ætheria's structures. Challies applied a little pressure to the two doors. They wouldn't budge. The stratoneum was solid, unyielding. But perhaps it could be forced.

Panting from the increasingly penetrating cold, Challies sat up and lifted the lantern to head height. He looked around the walls of the Larder. In Island Twenty-Three's warehouse—where the descent pods were stored—he knew there was a wall-mounted launch button to send the pods down. But here? Like an overstocked general goods store, every inch of the Larder's walls were lined with shelves overflowing with supplies for surviving in the stratosphere. But nowhere could he see a button or even a switch.

How did the maintenance crews get these open? Was there some master switch up above? Did they use their Nanokepp Cards? But even then, Challies saw no Nanokepp magnetic sensor anywhere in the room.

Challies grunted with disgust and stood.

If he was going to get out through the trap door, he would have to kick it open. But doing that without being secured was a sure way to fall. He looked around. The harnesses were there. The winches were there. The carabiners and climbing gloves were there.

Working quickly to stave off the cold, Challies walked over to one of the shelves and removed a rappelling harness. He set the lantern on the ground and, with trembling hands, held the harness outspread and threaded his feet through the two leg openings. He pulled it up to his groin over his AG suit and clipped the harness in the front. He squatted to check that all carabiners and tecton loops were securely fastened. With this done, he took a winch from the shelf and secured hooks to the front of his rig.

Satisfied, he stepped up to the edge of the maintenance hatch, his booted toes jutting out a few inches over the lip. With his left hand, he reached out and steadied himself against the solid vertical support wire. With his right, he clipped the winch on and sat down to make sure it held. It did. He could now lift his feet and hover above the trap door, his entire weight solidly held in place by the harness.

But Challies wasn't going to hang there idly, waiting for the ACF to burst in. He pressed the winch's release lever and slid down a foot. His feet now touched the trap door. He could even bend his knees and squat down, coming to a stop only when the attachment safety cable between the winch and his harness pulled taut.

Challies stood, the carabiners clinking as he moved. He took a deep breath. He squatted again.

And with a grunt, he exploded upward, jumping to the full length of the attachment cable, which snapped taut at his jerky movement. The cable yanked him back downward and, with legs together, he rammed his feet directly into the joint between the two trap doors.

Blam!

The doors trembled but remained closed. At the deafening sound, Challies winced. He turned and looked at the closed hatch cover he'd entered through. He froze, holding his breath. He listened. Had anyone heard? The only sound he could detect was that of the howling wind outside. Hearing this, he was satisfied any sounds he could make would be drowned out by the gale.

He clenched his teeth and jumped again.

Blam!

The doors wiggled.

Blam!

Blam!

Blam!

Blam!

Blam!

With each jump, he tried to kick harder. Despite the cold, he soon felt sweat dripping down his temples and under his chin. His muscles screamed from the effort, his bones were jarred from the impacts, and his breath came in shallower and shallower gasps. His muscles were running out of oxygen. And the more he asked of them, the weaker he became. Still, his hope remained kindled each time the doors wiggled in place. When his feet landed each time, he could tell the doors were held up by springs or hydraulics, and that the force of his kicks were slowly but surely straining them. Each time, the doors popped open slightly, only to snap back into place when he jumped back up.

Challies paused, out of breath. He clutched the support wire with his right hand. He placed his other on his bent knees. He leaned over and panted, trying desperately to fill his lungs and stave off hypoxia. Everyone in Ætheria knew that physical exertion led to lightheadedness—unless, of course, you were a member of the High Command, in which case you were allowed a personal supply of oxygen.

But that was not Challies.

When his head stopped spinning, Challies squatted down once more and hurled himself upward and then down.

Ka-crack!

This time, his feet landed squarely on the same side of the trap door's joint. With a pop and a hiss, one of the doors gave way and his feet slid out. Startled by his ground suddenly giving away, Challies scrambled to activate the winch. He snapped its lever to the downward position. The device engaged just as his rear landed on the trap door, his legs protruding through the open flaps.

The trap door didn't open completely. With their hydraulics still intact, the two flaps pushed back upward in an attempt to close. Their path, however, was blocked by Challies's thighs.

"Aaaahh!" he screamed as the mechanical doors pushed against his muscles. His voice echoed through the Larder and made his ears ring. The wind outside began to whistle violently, the gap in the doors creating a flute-like embouchure hole. The doors' hydraulics hissed, straining to close.

Safely harnessed in, Challies yanked his hands from the support wire and pounded against the doors, desperately trying to knock them open. With each blow, he felt them shudder; but in between efforts, he could feel them again pinch harder, as if they were determined to sever his legs midway between the knee and the hip. As he struggled, Challies had a vision of sliding backward from the closed doors with two mangled stumps, his blood leaving his body and forming a congealed puddle across the Larder's floor. He would bleed out. He would die. And then he would surely join the Cthonians in the morgue as yet another frozen specimen of an enemy of the state.

Challies pulled harder. But the doors were angled

slightly outward, forming two flattened barbs that pushed farther into his legs, gripping tighter with each attempt. The sensation in his feet and calves disappeared. He yanked and writhed. A searing pain shot through his thighs—it felt as though the doors were cutting into his skin.

"Ahhh!"

Realizing that he would lose his legs if he continued to struggle against the doors, Challies stopped moving. He was panting heavily, and he felt close to fainting from the pain and lack of oxygen. He once again gripped the wire and tried to calm his panicked heart. *Breathe, breathe, breathe . . .*

Challies relaxed his legs as much as his pumping adrenaline would let him. He planted his hands squarely onto the sides of the trap door. Slowly, carefully, gently, he turned and wiggled his legs in an attempt to twist them free. They slipped upward, but the doors quickly pinched into an uninjured portion of flesh, ripping his AeroGel suit. He thought he felt blood trickling down his insulated leg; but with his feeling gone, he wasn't sure. His head spun. He twisted his legs. He pushed. He pulled. He groaned. He wrenched. As he inched his way out of his trap, he had the impression that two large blades were shaving the muscles and skin from his legs, leaving nothing but a bare skeleton.

After what seemed like an hour of excruciating writhing, Challies had gotten his legs completely through, leaving only his booted feet wedged in the trap door. Strips of his AG suit hung down from different parts of his legs like large black banana peels. Underneath, his lacerated skin oozed blood into the shredded suit, while the biting cold gnawed at his exposed flesh.

With nausea and vertigo closing in, Challies screamed one last time and jerked his feet from the trap door, which snapped shut behind them.

Now free from his crushing trap, Challies sank into unconsciousness, his limp body hanging upside down from the Larder's maintenance harness.

FOUR

BERNUAC HQ WAS BUZZING. WHEN ROMAN arrived from his aborted pursuit, HQ's assembly auditorium was already packed with what must've been the entire Ætherian Cover Force of nearly two hundred scouts and Protectors. Roman knew the hall held more than two hundred people. Now it seemed ready to burst, with ACF standing in the aisles and in the back. Only the platform stage at the front was empty . . . empty but awaiting someone to address the crowd.

It was the middle of the night, but every scout was wide awake—too awake, even. Some stared ahead with empty eyes, stunned. Others chatted nervously among themselves, their hands wringing or wiping across the front of their AeroGel suits. An uneasy energy filled the room. Roman and his group of ten scouts, still pumped with adrenaline, wedged their way into the echoing room and along the back wall. No sooner had they stepped in from the frigid stratospheric night than anxious whispers surrounded them.

"Did you suspect anything?"

"He's gone missing, that's for sure."

"Why would he do this?"

"His card was used to cross the Zipp lines and access the warehouse."

"This is a Tossing, for sure. Maybe not even a trial."

"I can't believe it."

"Was he with them?"

"People only saw the boy and the Cthonian zipping over. Not him."

"Is *he* going to talk to us, do you think?"

"Have you ever heard of him talking to the ACF like this?"

"He is, he is. I just heard it from Schlott on the way in."

"If it's him, you know there's trouble."

"Him" meant only one person: the Head Ductor. Ever since Roman could remember, and especially since he joined the ACF, the Head Ductor was the only person in Ætheria anyone referred to only by a pronoun: he, him, his . . . never by name. In fact, Roman didn't even know the Head Ductor's name, though the rumor was that it was either Greg or Samsa. Of the two, Roman preferred to think his name was Greg. Samsa just seemed too bizarre.

Roman had seen the Head Ductor plenty of times, but only in hushed meetings with Ætherian High Command officials. And more recently, in highly confidential situation report meetings about the ongoing crisis. Physically, the Head Ductor was unimposing. A short man, he shuffled about on legs that seemed to have no knees. His frame looked bony and gaunt, though his face was strangely chubby. He peered out at the world through thick glasses that magnified his eyes, making him look like some giant, four-foot-tall cockroach. Because he always wore dark blue, his body even had the color of a bug, and his perpetually slicked-down black hair added to the effect.

But now? Was he going to talk to the *entire* ACF? Roman had never heard of the HD addressing everyone like this. And here? In the dead of the night?

Roman looked around at the hundreds of other scouts. Judging by their shifting eyes and unsure looks, they didn't know, either. Whatever was going to happen, Roman just hoped it would happen quickly. Because right now, the only thing spinning through his mind was that his quarry had gotten away. The Cthonian and that kid were now probably all the way down below, and with every minute Roman and his scouts wasted here in this meeting, the fugitives were getting farther and farther away.

As if cued by an invisible conductor, the room suddenly fell quiet. Off to Roman's left, someone cleared their throat. Roman's pulse beat in his ears. Around him, dozens of AG suits rustled. Their wearers shifted in place, trying to hold still so that they could listen.

And then there was a gasp as dozens of ACF scouts toward the front drew in their breath. They'd seen something just offstage that the rest of the room could not. Roman craned his neck to see. Like flowers stretching upward in a field, the other scouts did the same, stretching, looking. Their heads were turned to the left. Murmurs floated through the crowd.

"It's him!"

"I told you."

"Do you see him?"

"There he is!"

In the next instant, the whispers were broken by the sound of footsteps shuffling onto the stage. The room fell deadly silent. There, scurrying in from stage right, the Head Ductor appeared. He was dressed in a dark blue suit. His hair was slicked back, and his beady eyes filled his frames. Despite his puny stature, he walked with confidence—head erect, shoulders back. His jaw was clenched, and Roman thought he saw a glisten on the Head Ductor's forehead. Tiny veins traced meandering paths across his temples. He clutched a small piece of white paper in his right hand. Similar to Roman and the other members of the High Command, he wore a small container of oxygen on his back.

When he arrived at center stage, the Head Ductor stopped and faced the crowd. He scanned the hundreds of rapt heads, as if taking roll. Roman could see the Head Ductor's shoulders rise and fall as he breathed—one breath, two, three, four . . . What was he waiting for? There were fugitives on the loose! Didn't the Head Ductor know that? Didn't he know that with every second he waited, the Cthonian and Rex Himmel were getting farther and farther away? And who knows what they were planning? What if they had fled down below to plan some other attack? There was no time to lose, but yet . . . Roman cracked his knuckles behind his back. The noise caused a few scouts in front of him to turn and glare at him before turning back to the stage. Roman ignored them.

With a barely audible "Hmm," the Head Ductor turned to face the wings of stage right and nodded. A shuffle of feet emerged from backstage. The Head Ductor then cast his insect gaze on the crowd and spoke.

"These are difficult times . . . yes, difficult times for Ætheria."

Roman furrowed his brow at the Head Ductor's first words. He didn't remember the Head Ductor's voice being so high and squeaky. It almost sounded like he was deliberately trying to speak in an irritating voice. There was something nasal and grating about it—something almost inhuman.

"In just a week's time, the following has befallen us: Spies have come from below. Fortunately they have died here of hypoxia, but not before communicating with whomever would like to do us harm. And harm they did, striking out in a manner most heinous at our only source of water and cthoneum. We sent a group of Auscultors down to investigate. Five came up to report, but then the remaining scouts below were attacked. Most were killed. And then, one of *them*, a Cthonian," at the word, several dozen scouts hissed in disgust, "yes, a *Cthonian* came back up with our one remaining scout. And this scout, well, we had thought he would be loyal and truthful, but he has tried to sow lies about Cthonia in an attempt, no doubt, to sabotage us all." Another hiss rippled through the crowd. "And as proof of his perfidy, behold! Look at what he has done! He and the Cthonian have escaped from our Sanatorium, and now! Now they have fled below, no doubt to plan some further attack."

As the Head Ductor spoke, Roman marveled at how much the Head Ductor already knew. He could only conclude that all of his radio transmissions to Bernuac HQ or Tracker interceptions were being monitored directly by the Head Ductor. Either that, or Schlott or someone else from Bernuac HQ was communicating all developments immediately.

"My friends," the Head Ductor continued, "the situation is dire. Yes, we have two escapees and saboteurs. Yes, we have been attacked, *twice*. And yes, though we have been making rapid progress in repairing the Proboscis, we are out of time. The battle is just beginning. And why?" He paused and glanced around the crowd. Every scout seemed to be holding their breath.

"I'll tell you why!" he screamed, veins bulging. "It is because someone else has been helping them. Someone from inside our beloved community! *That* is why they have escaped! *That* is why we are threatened! *That* is why you are here now!"

As the Head Ductor spoke faster and faster, his shoulders began to heave and his face to pale. Before continuing, he took a few deep desperate huffs from the tube that stretched around his head and embedded itself into his nostrils. The color returned to his face. From his position at the back of the room, Roman had the impression that even the Head Ductor's eyes became clearer. As if breathing in the oxygen had strengthened his vision. Like a drug. The HD removed the tube from his nose, reattached it to the canister on his back, and continued. This time, he read from the sheet of paper he'd carried onstage.

"So." Roman noted that the Head Ductor's voice was less squeaky. "The facts are these: Two of our ACF Protectors were placed on duty to take Rex Himmel to the Sanatorium Complex. All procedures went as planned. Then, at approximately one o'clock in the morning—so, two hours ago—one of the Protectors was apparently attacked and dazed via Stær gun by another, Protector Challies 2496, who had returned to the Sanatorium after he and his partner had successfully reported the detainee transfer with Bernuac HQ."

Roman felt his temples burn at the Head Ductor's reference to him. At least the Head Ductor knew that Roman had done his job as he was supposed to.

But as the Head Ductor spoke, Roman scanned his memory of the previous day for any unusual behaviors on the part of Challies. No matter how hard he thought, he couldn't remember Challies doing or saying anything out of the ordinary. Still, Roman had gotten the sense that something about Challies was different, strange. Yes, he'd followed all standard operating procedures for transferring a suspect. Yes, he'd filled out the forms at the Sanatorium intake. Yes, he'd accompanied Roman to Rex's exam. But Roman *sensed* something different in his tone of voice, in his movements—they had seemed more jerky, less relaxed than normal. At the time, he'd let his feelings go because he'd known and worked with Challies for so long.

Things now seemed much clearer in hindsight.

At these thoughts, Roman felt a surge of panic:

Should he tell the Head Ductor what he'd sensed? Would he be investigated? Or did the Head Ductor think Roman had done his job as he should? He did say Roman had done his job *successfully*, didn't he? And after all, it was Bernuac HQ that had called him off the chase. Surely he couldn't report just a *feeling*?

What did the Head Ductor know?

"Upon cowardly attacking the boy's guard," the Head Ductor continued, snapping Roman out of his thoughts. "Protector Challies opened the detainee's door and made contact with him. Though what he said exactly, we do not know. What we *do* know is that upon doing this, Challies and the boy went to the Cthonian's room, whereupon he enabled the two to escape. Which they have done.

"Now, some of you may be wondering: what about the criminal's Tracker?" At the mention of the Tracker, Roman unconsciously shifted his right hand to his left wrist. There, his Tracker was attached, sending a steady stream of communication of his whereabouts to Bernuac HQ. It was one of the headquarters' jobs to monitor all scouts, at all times. "Well," the Head Ductor continued, "what we have also discovered is that, while on guard in front of the Cthonian's door, the criminal successfully removed his own Tracker, though how, we do not know yet. We discovered this when the emergency call was put through for the criminal and his partner to report immediately to apprehend the fugitives. When he did not report, a supervisor was sent and a search party went outside. And there, outside, at the southeastern edge of the Sanatorium building, we found this!"

With a flourish, the Head Ductor reached into his front pocket and withdrew a Tracker, which he held above his head. The Tracker's wristband had been severed midway. Challies must've clipped it. At the sight of the damaged device, an audible gasp filled the hall.

"This is the evidence that we have! Here is your proof!" he proclaimed. "And here is what else we know: any use of the Zipp lines is instantly noted. This is how we tracked the boy . . . Rex Himmel . . . " The Head Ductor seemed to struggle to say the name. "And we tracked the Cthonian to the descent pod launch warehouse. And what is more: because our scouts followed only *two* fugitives to the site, we know that they used the criminal's NanoKepp Card to get away. So, the traitor must have fled somewhere between his intervention at the Sanatorium and Island Twenty-Three. In other words, he is here. In Ætheria. And he is armed and considered highly dangerous. We have already lost our water and cthoneum intake. We cannot afford to lose anything else."

The Head Ductor paused and looked at his watch.

"It is now 03:21. At precisely 04:00 hours, you will each report to your unit Points. Assignments have already been made to monitor all Zipp line launch and landing pads. We will spread out. We will disperse, and we will comb every square inch of Ætheria's islands until we have found the traitor.

"In the meantime, we will prepare a ground assault force to secure the area around all supports and guy wires holding up Ætheria. We will be sending a force of two hundred ACF at once. But," the HD clenched his fists, crumpling the paper he'd been reading from, "to do this, we must wait for the weather to clear. If we send down so many, we will need to use the harness descents under each island. You would be exposed to the elements. And currently there is a thunderstorm directly below us. We must wait for it to pass.

"What is more, I have ordered more Stær guns to be prepared. Everyone will be armed. They are almost ready. When the storm has cleared, you will be going down *en masse*. And at the first sign of hostile forces, we will strike first in such a display of Ætherian fire and fury that those troglodytic Cthonians won't know what hit them. We've worked too hard, and we've not survived just to have our life force sucked away. We will win."

FIVE

MÁIRE WAS JUST GETTING INTO A RHYTHM at work when she was summoned. Back in her former life in Ætheria, every aspect of her existence had been defined by rationing: oxygen, water, electricity, heat, food, effort . . .

When she'd landed in Cthonia sixteen years before, her experience in allocating resources had made her an asset to Cthonia's water distribution plant, located deep in the belly of the behemoth cave the Cthonians had colonized. There, she and fifty other workers monitored water extraction from Cthonia's only identified aquifer—which, for the past two weeks, had been dry. Since then, the fifty-one workers spent their time managing Cthonians' usage of the remaining water stores. Their goal: to keep a catastrophe from becoming a disaster. They had enough for just less than a month . . . if they were careful.

"Máire?" a man's voice behind her made her jump. She turned from her spreadsheet, which she'd already audited and checked three times that morning. She was almost relieved to be able to turn away from the numbers.

"Yes?" she faced Steve Dunner, her direct overseer.

"How's it going?" he asked, his eyes darting over her sheet. Even though Máire had spent sixteen years communicating with the Cthonians, she was still not used to their accent, which sounded guttural and choppy. She'd often wondered how she sounded to them. At times she had to concentrate to follow what was being said.

"Okay. The numbers are working out. But nothing new, there."

"Yeah?"

"Uh-huh. Each day, I expect things to turn out wrong or some other problem to be there, but so far, so good."

"And the others?" Steve looked around at Máire's team. They were bent over worksheets, each tracking a different element of water extraction and distribution. Some focused on volume, some on mineral content, some on sanitation, some on filtration.

"No complaints." She shrugged. An awkward pause swelled between them. She sensed Dunner had something important to say, but he was hesitating. Because her work was so important, she began to feel uneasy at not working. She was also naturally jittery, and sitting still quickly stirred her anxiety. She squeezed her lips together and widened her eyes slightly as if to say, "Well?"

"Can you chat for a sec?"

"Sure? Here?"

"No, my section."

"Okay." Máire put her marker down and slid her files together. She instinctively turned them over, hiding the contents from any passersby . . . even though everyone who worked in her department knew what was on them. And they were the only ones likely to see anything she'd been doing.

The two walked a short, winding path to Dunner's office. Because space was so limited in the Cthonian Cave Complex, only overseers and members of the command were allowed quarters that could hold more than one person. In between offices and tubes, the complex looked like the interior of a massive dun anthill. Paths and channels wound here and there, up and down, with no right angles. Over the centuries of Cthonia's existence, the structures had been built up using clay mined from the cave's depths. Workers, normal citizens, overseers, and officials had all contributed to shape by hand the labyrinth of tubes and inhabited stalagmites.

Stairs had been formed into the sides of walls and the slopes of stacks of clay. Little, round windows like portholes dotted the walls and man-made stalagmites of the underground Cthonian complex. But the holes were not evenly spaced, as on a ship. They were scattered and irregular. The Cthonian cave looked like some artillery unit had used the structures for target practice, or like the entire compound had been fashioned out of hole-ridden cheese.

Like the others, Dunner's round station was cramped—not just by its small physical confines, but also by stacks and stacks of files piled so high that some were close to falling over. One glance at Dunner's office showed he'd been overwhelmed over the past few days. When Máire saw the backlogged work, she felt relieved that at least she was meeting all of her deadlines.

"Thanks for coming in," he said, working his way to a small desk in the corner. His chair was one of what the Cthonians called a *sterdh*—a seat sculpted into the wall from lumps of clay. Some people liked these and said they were the best available, since they conformed to the shape of your back. Máire hated them. She preferred more traditional chairs— the ones that followed the centuries-old designs from *before*. Dunner sat and pointed to a stack of files to the left of the door.

"You can just shift those around and make a seat. You won't hurt them."

"The files?"

"Yes. Just make a seat." His eyes smiled, but his mouth revealed no emotion.

Máire rumpled her forehead and turned to the left. She bent over a stack of files several feet high and lifted the top half, splitting the stack in two. She let the stack drop next to its bottom half. *Ploomp!* A few files wafted from the top and floated to the floor.

"Leave those," Dunner said with a dismissive wave. "I'll figure it all out later. Just try not to crush or rip anything." He stifled a chuckle.

"If you say . . . " She sat down on her improvised chair. "What's up?"

"So what are your thoughts about this whole thing?" he began.

"What, you mean the water situation?" She knew this wasn't what he was driving at.

"No, I mean . . . them. The Ætherians. You know things are heating up. People are dying. Our people."

"Yes, I know."

"So I needed to call you in because there's someone here who wants to talk to you. Not me, actually."

"Who is that?"

Dunner looked at some files on his counter as if trying to remind himself of the person's name.

"It's Caput Thomas Brun from command. He was with the group that went out and encountered the Ætherians. The flying brigade."

"Yes?" Máire asked, frowning.

"The ones who shot at us."

"Ah."

"And he wants . . . " Dunner was interrupted by a knock at his office door. He looked up. "That must be him. Come in."

The door opened and a plain-looking man walked in. He wore no uniform, only dark blue pants and a synthetic shirt. His hair was cut almost to the scalp. It was one of those haircuts designed to camouflage a balding head. The man's eyes were laughing, but deep bags underneath revealed a life of hidden worry.

"Ah," Dunner said. "Máire, Thomas Brun."

"Please. Call me Tom," he said, extending his hand. Máire took it and shook.

"Sorry," she said. "Should I salute or anything?" Her voice betrayed a hint of sarcasm.

Tom laughed an irritating, high-pitched laugh. "No, nothing like that. You're not a spotter, after all." He stepped into the office and looked for a place to sit. Seeing none, he plopped himself down on a pile of files in the corner. "How have you been?"

"Fine. Thank you." Máire couldn't hide her confusion. Her face suggested she suspected Tom of hiding his real intentions. In her sixteen years in Cthonia, she'd never seen him before. This didn't mean that she didn't automatically mistrust him. She just had no reason *to* trust him, beyond his rank.

"Look," he said. "I'll jump right in. We don't have a lot of time." He cleared his throat, shot a glance at Dunner, and continued. "When you first came here, you know, as an asylum seeker, did you tell the command anything about Ætheria . . . about *up there*? I mean, what it was like and how you ended up here? Did you describe the colony?"

"Well, yes. And I've been teaching it. Well, along with rationing water."

"Yes, that's right. So, yesterday I got a message from one of the members of Cthonia's governing council. They need some more information. From you."

"What? More than what I've already said? More than what I have been teaching, year after year?"

"Yes. This time they need a detailed map of Ætheria. And they need you to draw it. They need to know everything: how many islands there are, who lives where, where the command buildings are . . . everything. They want it to be to scale as much as you can remember after sixteen years. And they need it in three days. No less."

"A map? What for?" Máire's nerves tightened at Dunner's request.

"Well, let's just say we *need* it. And soon. But there's more. They need something else. From you."

"What?"

"Well, we need you to stop your work here. You'll need to join a team to go inspect the wreckage and explosion site where our water-seeking command was stationed."

"Me? But I'm not a spotter. You said so yourself."

"We know that. But you're the only person in all of Cthonia who knows anything specific about *up there*. We need you to try to make sense of the wreckage. Who knows? Maybe you can help us avoid any further conflict. Or if there is conflict, maybe you can help us make all the right moves."

"But wait, what about the fight? I heard about it on the news! Everyone's talking about it! Are you trying to get me killed? I didn't run away from up there only to be caught again in some cavalier adventure!"

"Yeah, I thought about that," Tom agreed. "And nice word, by the way." He smiled. "But they know what they're doing. My spotters, I mean. And this group will be armed—not like the ones who went out before. You see, we're sending in a ground force to secure the area and make sure no one else comes down. Any questions?"

Máire opened her mouth, but no words came

out. She glanced one more time at Dunner as if seeking his approval before saying anything.

"Actually, yes."

"Go ahead."

"Why hasn't anyone already gone over there? Investigated or whatever? That was a week ago. What have you been doing?"

"Good question. It took us a bit to suspect something was wrong. We got no answers to our communication transmissions. That's when we scrambled the search and rescue airship, but that airship wasn't equipped to deal with a hostile force. We needed reinforcements. Armed reinforcements. So they came back, restocked, checked and refurbished the airship, and are ready to go. This time, with you." He paused, his eyes glowering into hers.

"Okay." She nodded. "One more question."

"Yes?"

"What choice do I have?" she finally said.

"I guess you're right." Tom shrugged. "We'll leave just after three a.m. In the dark. Our goal is to get there just at sunrise, so we have the entire day to work in the light. The flight is just over two hours. Be ready to go. No need to wear anything special. We just need you to look at the mess and tell us what you can see—or if you can make sense of anything. The two Ætherians they were chasing are long gone . . . maybe even up top. We don't know. While you are looking at the wreckage, a patrol will scout the area. There shouldn't be any trouble."

With that, he stood and stepped out, leaving Máire and Dunner alone.

SIX

ARAL AND REX PLODDED WEST.

In the dark and without any lights, the two used the dim glow of the remaining fire to guide them. Though more than a week had passed since Tátea's Power Works was attacked, the wreckage still smoldered. Its orangish light was faint, but in Cthonia's black, cloud-strewn night, it served as a beacon.

Determined, the two moved steadily, keeping their hands outstretched to avoid walking into guy wires or support struts hidden in the night. The ground was flat enough they didn't need to feel its surface before putting their feet down. If not for the presence of the hundreds of wires and supports, they could have sprinted across the sand with no worry of falling or tripping. Though they both would have prefered to run now to put as much distance as possible between themselves and the descent pod, there was too much chance of running into a guy wire and being clotheslined.

And Rex couldn't afford another injury. Not when they had to get away, and fast.

"How do you feel?" Aral asked after the two had established a steady pace somewhere between a fast walk and a shuffle.

"Better. My shoulder and head still hurt, but better."

"Good. Ow!"

"What is it?" Rex asked.

"A wire. I'm okay. But be careful. They're everywhere."

"Yeah. Do you hear anything?"

"What do you mean?"

Rex took a deep breath. "Nothing," he said. "I'm just trying to keep my ears open. In case anyone comes down after us."

Without slowing her pace, Aral turned and looked behind them. She squinted through the dark, but shook her head and turned back around.

"I can't see anything," she said. "Can't hear anything either."

"Can we just walk? My head hurts too much to talk. I need to lie down."

"Do you need help?"

"No, I just . . ."

"Here," Aral said, stepping up to Rex and putting her arm around his torso. At the same time, she reached over with her other hand and guided his healthy left arm around her waist. Being a foot taller than he, she had to bend down to do this. Otherwise her arm would've draped over his shoulders. She latched her hand around the side of his waist and squeezed, lifting. Rex felt the load on his feet lighten. His steps came more quickly. As she lifted, he squeezed back, and felt the muscles under her shirt tighten and work with her long, Cthonian strides.

"Better?"

"Thanks. Yeah."

"Okay, let's get there."

Shuffling along at a faster clip, the two meandered through the night. With her long right arm, Aral swept through the space ahead of them, probing for guy wires or struts. Her shoulder still smarted from the wire that scraped her minutes before. She now didn't want to catch a wire in the face.

With no sounds coming from behind them, the two kept their eyes forward. With about five miles to cover between the descent pod landing area and the impact site, their first goal lay about two hours away. Still, Aral moved ahead cautiously, keeping her eyes peeled for any sign of the Cthonian forces that had opened fire on them and pursued them before. Rex also kept his eyes open, but his throbbing headache, combined with the searing pain in his shoulder, caused his vision to blur. Because of the dark, he couldn't notice much difference, but he was essentially walking blind.

As if reading Aral's mind, Rex broke the silence. "What do we do if we see them? The Cthonians."

Aral shrugged. The upward pressure on Rex's elbow caused him to groan.

"Surrender. That's all we can do. We're not armed. Not like before. And we're not going to shoot, that's for sure. So there's no reason for them to shoot at us."

"Let's hope."

"Let's."

Thirty minutes passed. An hour. An hour and a half. With each step, Rex's pain grew, and he soon realized that he was wracked by thirst. It wasn't a slight thirst—the kind you get after being in the sun for a little too long. No, this was a body-wrenching, agonizing thirst that turned his tongue into a lolling wad of cotton and his limbs into ashen sticks of bone and drying flesh. Was it his injury? The stress of everything? Whatever it was, his legs became heavier and heavier, to the point where Aral noticed his putting less and less weight on each step.

"I need to rest," he finally said, stopping his feet as if to make his point. "I've got to have something to drink. Anything." He looked around in the dark.

Aral relaxed her arm and stretched tall, peering westward. She could now see the first signs of the Power Works's embers. These were no longer just a glow hovering above the horizon. She could make out the mangled forms of the wreckage—the twisted and bent stratoneum struts and gnarled guy wires, the clumps of man-made earth, the shattered frames and foundations of Tátea's former power-generating building, and, here and there, shreds of the Cthonian command post tent where she'd worked with thirty other Cthonian spotters . . . right before they cut the Proboscis and found the Tátea Power Works crumbling down upon them. This was also where she'd first met Rex about a week before, when he and a group of other Ætherians had come down from above.

"I can see the mess," she said, shifting her gaze to Rex. In the faint glow of the remaining fires, she could tell that his eyes were lowered to the ground. "Look, let's just make it there. There's still an airship there. That's where I hid. Before. It'll give us shelter. Why don't we at least get there and you can rest inside? When you'd found me, I'd just found our water and food stores. They hadn't been destroyed or anything. But you surprised me. Maybe now I can find them in the dark."

Rex looked up. His eyes stung. He shook his head.

"Okay," he said, "but just let me lie down a bit here. Only for a few minutes, I swear. Then we can go. Just a few minutes."

Aral looked behind them, as if expecting a team of Ætherians to swoop down on them at any second. But all she saw was dark, followed by more dark. By now she was convinced no one was coming. She turned and faced forward. She squinted, peering towards the glow in search of Cthonian silhouettes—people who might be patrolling the wreckage site . . . the same ones who'd chased them earlier and killed most of the Ætherian team. People she might surrender to. But here as well, she saw that she and Rex were alone . . . alone in the middle of a disaster site. Still, she felt too exposed out in the open. It was dark, but she had the uncanny sense someone was watching them.

"No," she said, "we're almost there. It's too dangerous here, outside. In the dark. Come on." Without another word, she reached down and scooped Rex up. He moaned as she lifted, her left arm under his middle back and her right under his knees. Despite his pain, he couldn't help but be impressed by her strength. She hoisted him off the ground as if he weighed nothing at all.

"Can you hold your left arm out straight ahead? See if we're about to walk into any wires?" she asked.

"Sure." Rex avoided her eyes, even in the dark. The urge to smile was overwhelming, in spite of his thirst. He'd never met someone so strong before.

With Rex in her arms, Aral picked up speed. Rex waved his arm out in front of them like a bug's antenna. As they neared the wreckage, the orange light of the remaining flames, though dim, made it easier to see oncoming wires. Rex looked for vertical lines hovering in his field of vision. Lifting and dipping gently in her arms, he wondered if she saw the same thing.

After about twenty minutes, Aral arrived at the first twisted wires. She nimbly maneuvered through these and worked her way forward and to the left, where the smoldering wreckage thinned out. In the dim glow, Rex recognized the spot where he first spotted Aral a week ago. And now here he was, being carried across the impact site by someone he'd thought was an enemy. How much longer would she walk before tiring? No sooner had the question flashed through his mind than Aral answered him.

"The airship's not far . . . maybe a hundred meters or so," she said. Rex looked up and sensed she was stretching her neck for a better look. "There it is. We'll rest there until morning. I don't think anyone's around. If they were, they'd be on guard. But there's no one. Still, better to move during the day."

She looked down at Rex. The two made eye contact. "Do you think you'll be able to walk tomorrow?"

"It's not that. I need water. I've never been this thirsty before."

"Hmm. I'll tell you what: there's a hidden compartment in the floor of the airship. We can sleep there. We should be safe. You rest, and I'll see if I can find the water and food. I'll dig around."

"Thanks."

As Aral stepped up into the slumbering aircraft, the open, free sounds of outside gave way to metallic, claustrophobic echoes of an enclosed chamber.

Their breathing suddenly became audible, and each of Aral's movements seemed amplified tenfold.

"Shh!" Rex instinctively snapped after Aral had taken several steps into the plane.

"You've never been in one of these before, have you?" She chuckled softly and squatted, easing him to the floor.

"No. But it's not that. The noise!"

"It's nothing, just us moving around in here. It echoes. See? I can go look outside if you want."

Rex stretched his back and lay down. He tried to focus his eyes on the airship's ceiling, but dark filled his view. The only light in the hold came from the rectangle of the open door. Outside, the flames crackled and snapped, creating a flickering, orange frame to their self-made prison.

With careful steps, Aral worked her way through the plane's body, pausing here, bending over there, examining. She seemed to be inspecting every inch of the interior. Rex turned his head to follow her with his eyes. He couldn't tell what she was looking for. As if sensing his eyes on her, she stopped looking and faced him.

"Look," she said, shuffling through the dark to a place midway between where Rex lay and the tail of the plane. "Enough talking. We need to get you hid so I can go find some water. You need some. And we both will, soon. Here." She bent over and reached out her hands. In the dark, the scrape of her fingers over the metal floor gave Rex a chill. He tried to squint and make out what she was doing. But all he could manage was to find her lanky, black silhouette hunched over the floor.

With a metallic click and squeak, Aral turned a latch and lifted. A one-meter square trap door opened, revealing an even darker space beneath the floor of the plane's body. She let the door drop open with an ear-splitting clang.

"This is a cargo hold," she said. "Nothing too secret about it. But it's probably better to spend the night in here than just out in the open. We don't want just anyone walking in and seeing you. At least with this, only someone who knows about the trap door will have the idea to look down there. I hope."

Rex sat up and slid across the floor to the open door. He eased his lower legs in, but stopped before lowering his body through.

"Should I just stay here?"

"Yes. I'll close the door and go see what I can find. I'll try to find some water for you, and maybe anything else that can help. By foot we've got a few days ahead of us to get to my people. We need to be ready."

"Okay," Rex said, placing his hand on the edge of the trap door. "How deep is it?"

"Just jump. It's not that deep."

Rex slid his rear off the floor and into the void. His feet fell little over a foot before connecting with the plane's hard underbelly. Steadying himself with his hand, he lowered himself into the hold. Before disappearing below, he paused, his head bobbing in the dark like a ball on water.

"How long will you be?" he asked, trying to hide fear in his voice.

"I don't know. I'll hurry. No matter what, I'll head back when it starts to get light."

"What if you don't find anything?"

"You mean water?" She sighed and paused, lost in thought. "Without water, we're dead. We have to find some."

With that, she lowered the trap door over Rex's head and let it latch in place with a *click*.

———

Nearly a week had passed since Aral had last approached the smoldering wreckage of her team's command post. Then, she'd been overwhelmed by the emotion of everything that had happened. Not only had her entire Command Post been destroyed through her general's brashness, but she'd lost a close friend and a group leader whom she'd come to like and respect. Since they were young girls, she and Estrella had studied together, gossiped together, played together, and learned to ride eqūs together. Of all the people in her team, Estrella had known Aral the best. She'd been the one in whom Aral had confided her worries about Brondl's behavior. She'd been the one Aral would talk to late in the night about plans, hopes, and dreams. And she'd been the one who'd convinced Aral to join the spotters in the first place. And now she was gone. Through no fault of her own. And Tell? He'd looked after Aral, helped her, trained her, and believed in her. On more than one occasion, he'd stuck up for her in front of Brondl. With Estrella, Aral had lost a friend; with Tell, a mentor.

She felt alone. Exposed. In danger.

After she'd emerged from the airship following the explosion, she'd been too stunned to register her feelings. But now that things had cooled down at the scene, she fought with the pain of her loss, coupled with the need for her and Rex to survive. They both had their wounds, and now they were together. They had to support one another. And more importantly, now . . . now that Rex was injured and depending on her, she had to keep her own wits about her and not let her emotions blind her to what needed to be done.

She had to take control, and keep control.

When the Ætherians had found her before, she had just unearthed the rigid container that held their water and food stores. It had miraculously not been destroyed in the explosion, and it had contained enough food and water to get her entire ten-person reconnaissance team back the two days to the Cthonian Cave Complex. There would definitely be enough condensed fungus cakes and concentrated water blisters for her and Rex.

If the supplies were still there.

As she slunk forward in the dark, she kept her ears peeled for any sounds beyond the slight popping and crackling of fires that still smoldered beneath the wreckage. Squinting, she could make out only the vague forms of the pile of debris up ahead, as well as the ghostly silhouette of the airship that slumbered behind her. When she and Rex had arrived here minutes ago, her main concern had been the Cthonians who had fired on them before. But as she suspected, the area seemed empty of any humans. The airship must've returned to the CCC, most likely to fetch reinforcements.

Moving from memory rather than sight, she worked her way to where she knew the supplies lockers to be. Hearing nothing unusual, she walked faster, all the while easing her feet forward nimbly to avoid tripping. Though the pile still smoldered, she could see no orange or yellow flicker from the fires. They were hidden, buried deep in the wreckage.

As she approached the tapering southern end of the rubble, she sensed something she hadn't noticed before. The closer she got, the more she became surrounded and then engulfed by a powerful stench that seemed to be clinging to the rubble like a dense fog. It was like nothing she'd ever smelled. It was rancid, sour, putrid, and overwhelming. She soon had to cover her mouth and nose with her hands, but even that wasn't enough. She pinched her nose and breathed through her mouth. She gagged. She coughed. Her eyes watered. But she kept moving.

Up ahead, Aral could just make out the oblong, rectangular blackness of the supplies lockers. Her heart jumped at the sight, and in her excitement she almost forgot the stench. She rushed forward and knelt, returning to the precise spot where the ACF scouts had found her before. Her breath accelerating with adrenaline, she unlatched and lifted the clamped lid, and reached in with her left hand. She kept her right clamped onto her nose.

Relief flooded her. To the left side of the container, she felt dozens of soft, ball-shaped blobs, which she knew to be concentrated water blisters. Consuming just one of these would provide one person enough hydration for an entire day of hard effort. She then shifted her hand to the right, and couldn't help but giggling giddily as she wrapped her fingers around a pile of condensed fungus bars—high-powered energy snacks made from the CCC's edible fungus farms deep underground. These, as well as the water, were enough to get them both back to the CCC, assuming she could now figure out a way to transport the food and water without eqūs.

She craned her neck and looked around. Surely the animals had fled by now? After all, more than a week had passed since Brondl had destroyed their entire command post with his brash attack. She felt certain they would be long gone by now—no doubt searching for food elsewhere. But water? The animals had to be dead. Everyone in Cthonia knew that there was no water around except in deep aquifers.

But then she heard something.

Her muscles tensed and her nerves tingled with growing panic. *What was that?* Just feet from where she sat crouched, something moved within the pile of rubble—something right in front of her.

She lifted her eyes and peered at the pile. In the gloom, all she could make out was the irregular black-and-gray forms of shattered bits of stratoneum and tecton. By now, her eyes had adjusted more to the dark, and she could distinguish individual forms.

A rustle.

Something was moving. Then the thought struck. *What if someone's still alive in there?*

But it's been a week. She checked herself, still frozen with her eyes forward. *There's no way . . .*

Another rustle. A crack. Metal sliding against metal.

Riveted to her spot, Aral watched as the pile shifted in place and flattened out, sending bits of debris falling at her feet. She breathed a sigh of relief. The wreckage was merely shifting as bits continued to burn and collapse deep inside.

With a final *swoosh*, the six-foot-high mound completely deflated, sending a small cloud of dust wafting out over her. Coughing, she covered her mouth once again with both hands. She stood up as several more bits tumbled out, including a larger piece that seemed lighter in color and almost round. It rolled to her feet and tapped her ankle, coming to rest. She looked down and screamed.

She was staring at a human skull.

———

"How's that? Better?" Aral asked as Rex finished two water blisters and three fungus bars. He chewed slowly in the dark and swallowed.

"Much. Thank you."

Rex sat up and stretched his left arm. His wounded right arm tingled in its sling, a dull pain radiating from his shoulder to the rest of his body. The water blisters had an immediate effect—partly because he had been dehydrated, partly because the water was so concentrated. He felt revived and even invigorated. His headache calmed almost instantly. Feeling the life-giving water course through his system reminded him of the invigorating effect he'd first felt upon breathing the dense Cthonian air after years living in a permanent state of hypoxia.

After he'd finished eating and drinking, Rex looked at Aral's black silhouette.

"You okay?" he asked.

"Me? Yes, better. Especially now that we're down here."

"What happened up there? What did they want?"

Aral sat down and stretched her back. As she spoke, she kept leaning back to peer through the dimly lit doorframe. She must've seen or heard nothing. Each time, she sat back and continued talking.

"They tortured me," she said.

"Who?"

"I don't know. One looked like she was some military person. The other was a short man with glasses."

"Do you think it was the Head Ductor?"

"The who?"

"The Head Ductor. Of Ætheria. I've seen him a

few times, but not close up. He slicks his hair back and wears glasses. He's a small man. Even smaller than the rest of us . . . especially compared to you."

"Whoever he was, the woman kept looking at him. They cut my oxygen. I couldn't breathe. I kept passing out, but they wanted to know why Cthonia attacked. I told them what I knew. I don't think they believed me. I think they thought I was hiding something. They also wanted to know why your group was attacked down here. By the airship."

"Did you get a sense of what the Head Ductor really wanted? I mean, the man with the glasses?"

"Him? No, well, not much besides whether the Cthonians were going to attack or something like that. I think he's convinced that we're planning some kind of war. But that can't be. I think my people would want to talk to me if they knew I was alive. But I *do* think that man . . . the Head Ductor, I mean, might suspect you of something. It's just the way they acted when I mentioned you, or talked about when you and I came up in the pod."

"Hmm. They questioned me as well," Rex said, "but no torture. It was Deputy Head Schlott—the same person, I bet, who talked to you. The woman. She kept acting like what I was saying about the air here was some kind of lie. Like I was trying to spy or something up there. Like they thought *I* was the bad guy. And they kept watching me, too, with this Tracker on my arm. Everyone in the ACF wears them. But one time I took a little too long to do a job, and this voice came over like they always had their eyes on me."

SEVEN

MÁIRE TRIED TO HIDE HER EMOTIONS AS SHE was led to Cthonia's only remaining functional, on-site aircraft. As far as Cthonian intelligence knew, the only other airship was still parked at the site of the explosion, out in Cthonia's badlands. And because the entire company of spotters sent to find water had been killed, no one knew if that aircraft still worked.

The only time she'd ever laid eyes on the machines was when she'd arrived sixteen years earlier. Then, she'd glimpsed the behemoths resting outside of Cthonia's cave entrance. At the time, she didn't even know if they worked. Because of Cthonia's continual acidic rains, a massive, hangar-like shelter had been constructed to protect them. Even then, Cthonia's workers had to scrub the planes daily to remove corrosion caused by the lingering acidity in the air.

According to rumor, the airships were leftovers from hundreds of years before, when Cthonia first developed its civilization. And through the constant care and attention of generations of mechanics, they were kept functional . . . at least theoretically. Prior to the two recent missions, the last time they had been flown was more than fifty years earlier. Their parts had been kept lubricated, but doubts still remained about their reliability. Some said they were little more than expensive museum relics. Some said they would fall from the sky as soon as they took off. Some called them death traps.

Still, the two airships had just flown without incident, and this had silenced some of the rumors.

That morning at three a.m., while it was still

dark and chilly, Tom had met Máire outside of the CCC main entrance. When she'd spoken with him before, he'd been smartly dressed, but now he was fully uniformed and armed with some sort of machine rifle. He briefed her as they walked. She shifted her eyes from Tom's uniform to the airship. He wore a dark-blue collared shirt and pants, and a belt loaded with closed pouches girdled his waist. A small blue utility hat rested on his head.

"Looks like you've never flown before," Tom said, holding his hat down with his right hand and steadying his rifle sling with his left as he walked. "But then again, how many Cthonians have?"

Máire said nothing.

"Don't be worried. Some people think these planes aren't reliable because we never use them. But we just took both out on sorties, and there were zero mechanical issues. Since this one came back, it's also been fully checked out by our mechanics and engineers. I think you'll actually like it. When we go in, I'll show you a seat, and we'll need to strap you in."

"Strap me in? What for?"

"When the airship flies, sometimes it hits wind or air that can make it bounce around. We don't want you getting thrown around in there, now do we? Especially with all the weapons my spotters will have."

Máire looked at the airship, which was whining and hissing as it stirred to life. A massive engine clung to each wing. Just glancing at the machine, she couldn't understand how it flew. The engines looked like two huge but stubby ducts that pointed upward, perpendicular to the wings. They also looked like they could hinge on the wings, which would allow them to point forward and in line with the plane's body. A flurry of activity swirled around the rumbling aircraft. People Máire had never seen before were rushing up to the wings, the wheels, the body, and the tail. Each carried a clipboard, and each appeared to be checking some detail of the airship. They all wore bulky headphones, but she couldn't understand why. The airship was noisy, but not uncomfortably noisy.

"So this is the same airship we used six days ago when me and some of our spotters encountered hostile Ætherian forces. It's been all over the news, of course. We don't fly much, but when we do, the airship does what we need. Then, there were no mechanical problems, except . . . " his voice trailed off.

"Except what?"

Tom faced her squarely. "Well, they shot at us, didn't they? We could've been killed." Tom shook his head in disgust.

Máire turned her head towards Tom. "Were you on that . . . were you there? With them?" She hesitated, not knowing how best to ask.

"Yeah. It was scary. Real scary. We'd gone out to investigate the crash when the pilots saw this group. And the next thing we knew, we were being shot at. It was awful. Luckily none of us were injured. Still, the airship wasn't even hit."

"Do you know anything about the crash? The explosion? I mean, an Ætherian building fell from above, right, causing an explosion below?" Máire asked.

Tom shook his head. "No. That's why you're here, to tell *us* what happened. Or at least as far as you can tell from the rubble out there."

Máire frowned and stared straight ahead. At the rear of the plane, a massive cargo door opened and rested on the ground, forming a ramp. No sooner had it settled into place than dozens of armed spotters—both women and men—appeared from the other side of the airship and ran-marched up the ramp and into the aircraft, disappearing. Each carried the same kind of weapon as Tom's on their shoulder. They were black and metallic, with a threatening-looking tube extending out front. Following the spotters were three groups of other, unarmed Cthonians, but they were carrying just as many huge containers with the words FORENSICS—BIOHAZARD stenciled on the sides in yellow.

Máire remembered seeing armed spotters like these when she'd first been found by a Cthonian patrol years ago. But she hadn't seen any since. In all her years working on Cthonian rationing, she'd rarely stepped back outside, much less had any reason to encounter someone who was armed.

Máire's stomach tightened—not so much from fear of getting in that horrible machine and flying, but of what she might see in the wreckage. When she'd left Ætheria, she'd sworn she'd never again go back up, despite the pain she felt every day for leaving her son behind. Not a day went by that she didn't think about him: What did he look like now? Was he athletic, as she had been when she was that age? What was his character like? Stubborn, like her, or anxious and paranoid, like his father? Had his handicap affected him? Did other kids make fun of him because half of his face was paralyzed, making his facial movements lopsided? But more than all of this, she couldn't stomach the nagging worry that somehow he'd been in the building that had been destroyed and tumbled to Cthonia. Based on what she'd learned from the news and Tom, the building that had fallen had been Ætheria's Power Works. And she knew that Rex's foster dad had worked there. Could Rex have been there as well? Could he have been following in his foster dad's professional footsteps? The thought made her sick with worry.

"This way," Tom said, pulling her from her thoughts. He held his hand out toward the back of the airship, which gaped open at them like a giant beast ready to swallow them up. With the spotters inside, Máire and Tom were the only two left to board.

Máire shielded her eyes with her left hand and peered into the airship's rear. The spotters were already seated on both sides of what looked like a massive holding area that could probably fit more than two hundred people. Their backs were against the plane's sides, and their legs pointed toward the middle and toward each other. There were about forty or so, Máire couldn't tell. But she could see that all of their pale faces were turned toward her, watching. Some of the spotters seemed to have the hint of a smile as she stepped onto the ramp. These weren't mocking smiles. The spotters seemed to be encouraging her with their eyes.

Two steps behind Tom, Máire clumped up the metal ramp and into the dark interior, lit only by a red light and a dozen or so round windows at the spotters' backs. The men said nothing as she walked past, but Máire noticed they lowered their eyes at her presence. Why? Were they afraid of her? She'd never gotten used to the Cthonians making comments about her darker Ætherian skin and her shorter stature. But the Cthonians had always been open in their curiosity, never mean or cruel. Perhaps the spotters were reacting this way because her trembling legs and hesitation clearly showed she'd never flown before. She decided to say something to ease the tension.

"Don't all get up at once. It's just a little hard for me to come in with all these weapons I'm carrying."

A few chuckles replied. As Máire took her seat toward the front of the plane, she noticed some of the spotters shifting their rifles between their legs, as if embarrassed. She nodded and tried to force a smile, but the spotters turned to each other or pretended to adjust something on their gear belts. She felt out of place—not just because she was the only Ætherian among them, but also because she'd never touched a weapon in her life, and yet here she was surrounded by enough firepower to overwhelm the entire Ætherian Cover Force with their puny, almost laughable electric Stær guns . . .

Rather than sit across from her, Tom wedged himself into the last seat on their side—the right side—and pulled the shoulder straps and waist belt over his body. *Click.* He fastened the metal clips and nodded for Máire to do the same.

"They're not very comfortable, I know," he said. "But they'll keep you safe."

Máire nodded and strapped herself in.

"How long?" she asked.

Tom looked at his watch. "Not too long by air. Maybe two, maybe three hours."

"That's all? I remember the support structure was ages away."

"Oh, yes. Remember, back then you were on foot. Sure, if you walked it would take several days. Assuming you stopped at night as well."

"Oh!" Máire shouted as the plane's engines outside whined and sputtered to life. The entire airship shook and vibrated. The sound grew from a hiss to a whistle to a roar. The only time she'd ever heard anything this loud was when she'd taken one of the descent pods down from Ætheria to escape. As the pod had moved through the Welcans cloud, a thunderstorm had caused the entire vessel to shake and tremble—so much so that Máire had thought the pod might break loose from the support wire and fall to Cthonia. Several peals of thunder had even rattled her to the bone. Now, Máire instinctively jammed her fingers into her ears, as long-forgotten visions of the shaking and trembling descent pod flashed in front of her mind's eye. She glanced at Tom, whose eyes stared straight ahead but focused on nothing in particular. He seemed lost in a trance.

With a lurch and another ear-splitting roar, the airship shifted in place. And in the next second, they were airborne. As if hanging by a wire, the airship hovered for several seconds. It rotated counterclockwise, as the pilot positioned the nose away from the Cthonian Cave Complex and toward the open desert. When the airship stopped rotating, it hovered once more for a few seconds. Then, with a whine and a growl, it inched forward, gathered speed, and slowly worked its way out of the hangar and skyward.

The team headed east . . . toward whatever was left of Tátea's Power Works and the Cthonian water-seeking expedition.

EIGHT

WHEN CHALLIES AWOKE, HIS LEGS AND back screamed in pain—his legs, from being nearly mauled by the powerful Larder trap door, and his back, from hanging backward in his harness during his unconsciousness. As he stirred, he lifted his head and looked around, blinking at the white light of the lantern, which was still casting its angular glow over the Larder shelves. *How long was I out?* he thought, wiggling his toes to restore sensation. He reached across to his torn legs and fingered his wounds. The blood had fully congealed. He'd been out for more than an hour. It was time to move.

Challies reached up, grabbed the support cable with his right hand, and pulled.

With his head suddenly right-side up, Challies's vision danced with blackened dots that swam about. He clutched the cable with both hands, not wanting to faint once more.

When his vision had returned to normal and his head had stopped spinning, Challies unbuckled himself from the winch. His feet dropped onto the trap door, which wiggled only slightly. Seeing this, Challies felt a momentary surge of panic; but he now knew that it would take much more than his body weight to cause the doors to open.

He wouldn't fall to his death after all.

Challies stepped off of the trap door and writhed his way out of the harness, wincing in pain as it brushed the scrapes lining his partially bare legs. He tossed the tecton apparatus to the ground with a *clunk* and hesitated, massaging his legs. When the sensation had returned to his limbs, he turned and stepped over to the supply shelves. Working quickly and with trembling hands, he snatched a folded AG suit from a lower shelf and let it unfurl on the ground before him. He tore at his own partially shredded suit, pulling it from his tingling body. The frigid air bit at his exposed skin. With puffs of condensation swirling around his head with each out-breath, he worked his battered legs into the new suit, which was a size too small. He winced as it pressed against his scrapes. As he got the suit up and over his shoulders, he wondered that his legs had not gotten frostbitten from having parts exposed. But then, the AG suits' insulation was so strong that the areas surrounding any exposed skin would maintain their warmth, preventing significant damage to unprotected areas. That is, assuming the openings in the suit were not wider than one or two inches. And luckily, his weren't.

With the suit pulled tight and zipped Challies reviewed all of the options he had for attempting an escape. He couldn't stay here. He couldn't use the maintenance harnesses. He couldn't hide in Ætheria's buildings. He took a deep breath.

His only choice was to follow Aral and Rex.

And hope.

Challies worked his way to the metal ladder leading back up to the hatch and out into the night. He knew he couldn't make it out by rappelling down the support wire. He also knew that going back up top was risky. He needed to keep them moving, and he needed to get out. The ladder was the only way.

What he didn't know was what kind of fight was waiting for him up above.

Lantern in hand, he worked his way slowly and carefully up six of the rungs and tilted his head towards the circular latch he'd come through earlier. He steadied his breath, opening his mouth to avoid making any noise as he breathed. When he'd first run to the Larder entrance, he'd heard all sorts of noises: feet stomping, ACF scouts shouting and answering, clumps, beeps, alarms, and the occasional crack of static as someone radioed, no doubt, to

Bernuac HQ. As soon as he was inside, it became impossible to make out specific words because of the incessant wind and because of the thickness of the metal Larder cover. At most, he could make out only human noises. But now, he noticed something different. He heard only the wind. No voices. No footsteps. No radios. Nothing.

What was happening? Were Aral and Rex still alive? Had they been caught? A surge of panic filled him as he realized: if they hadn't been caught, why would everything be quieting down? Had he failed? He knew that if they had gotten caught, they would be Tossed. And him? He had helped them. He had cut off his own Tracker. He had given them his NanoKepp Card.

Even if the two were dead, he was a target.

What to do? If the ACF *had* captured Aral and Rex, their guard just might be relaxed enough for him to escape. Because if he was going to survive, the only way he could do it would be to slide over the Zipp lines by hand and make it to the descent pod warehouse. At least that was just one island away. And to do this, he'd need the ACF scouts' guard to be relaxed. It was the only way.

And then he remembered something: it was a new moon tonight; only the glint of the stars could betray him.

Confident in his decision, he tilted his head once more toward the metal slab and listened. Nothing . . . nothing but the howling wind.

Challies clicked off the lantern, plunging the Larder into darkness. He tossed the lantern aside; it clanked onto the floor. Feeling his way in the dark, he shifted his hand to the right side of his belt and felt around for his Stær gun's switch. With a click and a high-pitched buzz, the holstered weapon came to life. He looked down and saw the device's green on light shining back at him like a lone eye peering through the night.

Gripping the ladder's top rung with both hands, Challies lifted his shoulders, while at the same time lowering his head. Like Atlas lifting the world, he slowly thrust his shoulders into the round metal slab and, using both his legs and his arms, worked the manhole cover loose. His muscles soon screamed with the effort—not from the weight, but from the extreme slowness. He couldn't afford to make a sound, despite the gale-force wind outside.

A blast of frigid air stung his face. He took in a deep, stunned breath. Inhaling the fresh night air made him realize just how stagnant and humid the air in the Larder was—despite its cold. Even though oxygen at this altitude was extremely thin, it vivified him and stirred him more fully alert than he'd been in the past two days.

Slowly, slowly, slowly he lifted the manhole cover. The inch-wide opening was soon wide enough for him to turn his head and peer out.

Compared to the enclosed, pitch-black Larder, the bluish glow of the stars seemed almost blinding. Despite their pallor, he quickly realized that he'd been right: the moon was absent. Hopefully he would be all but invisible.

From his vantage point, Challies couldn't see the Zipp line launch pad. But he knew it was just around the corner of the Sanatorium's northern face, the corner of which now glowed eerily in the starlight. This was one of the only islands in Ætheria that held only one building. All of the others were covered with residential zones or clusters of Council or public buildings. And connecting these were winding networks of translucent polymer tunnels, forming what looked like a giant tubed complex above the clouds. But here, all Challies could see was the edge of one building that stood ten yards away like a wall. Beyond that, only the flat expanse of artificial ground turf reflected the lonely stars.

Challies hesitated, balancing the cover on his shoulders. Moving carefully, he rotated his head so that he could see in all directions. Turf, wall, and the emptiness of the night . . . he saw no people. The Sanatorium's exit door was closed. And more importantly, he saw no ACF scouts.

His passage was clear.

With a final heave, he eased the metal slab up and stepped up one rung on the ladder. As he pushed with his legs, pain shot up from the lacerations striating his thighs. Despite the pain, he slid his torso to one side and tilted his shoulders. The cover slid onto the turf above with a hollow thump. He jumped at the noise and looked up, instinctively drawing his Stær gun. Did anyone hear? Was anyone coming? The stratospheric wind whipped around him, making his ears sting. He saw no one. He stepped up and hobbled out of the hole.

With his feet planted on the Ætherian turf, Challies took one more look around. The Zipp line platform was about thirty or forty yards to his left, but it was hidden from him by the corner of the Sanatorium. Straight ahead, the island's edge cut through the darkness beyond in one straight, grayish line. Challies shuddered. Because the Sanatorium Complex was situated on the northern edge of the Ætherian archipelago, there were no islands beyond the edge and no Zipp lines. There was also no guardrail, which was typical on the residential islands. Here, one slipup would result in a plunge into the void . . . a minute-long drop before punching through the toxic Welcans cloud, then emerging beyond for another minute-long fall before slamming into the Cthonian soil at three or four hundred miles per hour. Back in ACF training, he'd learned that a fall from that height would result in bones' instant pulverization and organs' instant rupture, with blood oozing under the skin and among the organs. Rumor was that you'd be dead from a heart attack well before impact. But no one knew for sure.

This was what had happened to Challies's brother Abel nearly ten years ago. And this was the risk he now ran if he failed.

Challies shook off these troublesome thoughts. *No time for any of that,* he told himself as he turned left and led with his Stær gun. *Get distracted now, you die.*

Challies limped slowly, placing his feet down

on the balls and rolling into each step, wincing as the frigid air bit at his exposed gashes. Because the turf was slightly cushioned, he could probably have jumped up and down with no sound. But he was taking no chances, and his wounds kept him from truly entertaining such a thought. *Step, step, step* . . . he neared the building's corner and eased his head around the edge, eyes directed towards where he knew the Zipp line platform to be anchored twenty yards away.

He froze.

There, silhouetted against the night, he saw the form of what must've been an ACF scout. The figure was standing just inside of the Zipp line platform with his legs shoulder-width apart and his hands clasped in front of his waist. Or were they behind his back? Challies squinted. Here, the background was a bit lighter, since the descent pod warehouse floated about fifty yards beyond this northwestern edge of the Sanatorium Complex. The two were connected by the taut Zipp line. Despite the change in scenery, Challies couldn't tell who the person was or which way he was facing. One thing was certain: this was a guard who'd been stationed here to monitor all Zipp line activity. Was there one on the other side? If there was, they were too far away for Challies to tell.

So the Zipp lines are guarded, Challies thought. *Then the ACF is on to something. Because no one ever guards those. Either they've caught Aral and Rex and are looking for me, Aral and Rex are at large somewhere, or they've made it down and the ACF is looking for me.*

Because Challies could make out the gray hue of the turf, the building, and the guard, he assumed the person could see the same thing. And so the guard would definitely see Challies if he stepped out into the open. *Should I try to hit him with my Stær gun?* The guard was in range, with a Stær gun's effectiveness reaching just beyond fifty yards. *But the wind?* Challies quickly decided that taking a shot both from behind cover and against the wind would be too risky. He normally would not hesitate to fire in such wind, but he was worried he wouldn't be able to pull off a decent shot without exposing himself further. It pained him to daze another ACF scout or Protector, as he had done with Roman back in the Sanatorium. But right now he had to wrestle any feelings of guilt under control; one hesitation here could get him killed. And he had to get out.

Challies froze, keeping his eyes on the guard. He shifted his gaze to the man's waist, where his Stær gun would be holstered. Knowing that it was more effective in low light to look with his peripheral vision, he shifted his line of sight just to the right of the guard's waist. He was looking for the green glow of the weapon's on light. He held his breath and let his eyes relax. Nothing—only a black silhouette. Was the guard's Stær gun turned off? If so, maybe Challies would have a chance to rush the guard and overtake him. Assuming he could power through the pain and growing frostbite that was latching onto his exposed skin. If not . . .

A burst of adrenaline flooded Challies's veins as the guard suddenly moved. Without warning or a sound, the guard bent over and lowered his hands to his left leg. What was he doing? Scratching? Whatever it was, Challies now saw that the guard had been facing the island. His back had been to the Zipp line.

Seeing his chance, Challies sprang.

In an explosion of movement, he burst from behind the Sanatorium wall and sprinted toward the guard. High on adrenaline, he felt no pain; his legs did not fail him. Time seemed to slow for Challies as he pumped with his arms and legs, running as fast as he could. What in reality took only two seconds felt like minutes.

Surprisingly, the guard heard nothing until Challies was nearly upon him. Hearing the rustle of an AeroGel suit above the screaming wind, he jerked his head up from his leg, only to see the blurry form of his attacker. As he covered the last five yards to his target, Challies dropped his Stær gun to the ground and jumped. Only in this explosive movement did Challies scream from the pain that throttled his legs. In a panic, the guard shot to his feet and reached for his own weapon. It was too late. Challies leaned his head down, extending both arms in front of him, and landed a double-punch to the guard's chest that struck with the full force of his sprint.

"Ugh!" the guard groaned a breathy cry as the wind was pummeled from his lungs. He tumbled over backward onto the stratoneum Zipp line platform. A dull metallic thump pierced the wind as his bony arms and legs collided with the metal, his head bouncing violently as he landed on his back. Though stunned, he frantically snatched at his belt in an attempt to draw his Stær gun.

Winded but back on his feet, Challies glimpsed the deadly green light at the guard's waist. Without clearly seeing what he was doing, he brought down his right foot as hard as he could, aiming it directly for the light. His booted sole crunched on top of the guard's arm, pinning it to the platform.

"Ah!" Challies screamed in agony and terror. In the next instant, he drove his fist straight into the dark mass that was the guard's head. A searing pain shot through his fingers and hand at the impact. The guard made no noise at the blow, but his body became limp. Challies then planted both palms into the guard's side and pushed him toward the platform's far edge. His head, arms, and legs bounced a few times against the stratoneum before his body came to a rest inches before tumbling off into the void.

Challies paused, his breath wheezing as hypoxia loomed, threatening. He sat up straight, as if pondering what to do. Then, unexpectedly, the image of his dead brother flashed before his eyes, and he was filled with rage—rage against the Head Ductor for killing his brother. And rage against every person in this God-forsaken colony who blindly followed orders without realizing that the HD was strangling them all in his paranoia and lust for oxygen. Blinded by wrath, Challies sat on his rear and, using his battered legs, shoved the guard over the edge with his feet.

Now you know what it's like to be Tossed, he thought.

With white spots dancing in front of his eyes, Challies looked up. He felt a wave of nausea at the thought that he may have just killed an innocent man—perhaps someone who, like him, was also fed up with everything that was happening in Ætheria. Combined with the disgust at his actions was the sudden realization that, in pushing the guard over, he'd not thought to remove the man's Nanokepp card. If he'd only done that, he would be able to Zipp across with no difficulty, and perhaps even access the descent pod warehouse. How could he have been so blinded by his panic to escape that he'd missed such an obvious chance?

He turned and retched, but nothing came out— only air and the reek of stale gastric acid. Biting his tongue to fight his emotions, Challies looked up and shook his head as if to shake the thoughts away. Squinting, he tried to follow the Zipp line through the dark with his eyes, but at only ten yards out, everything became a jumble of blacks, grays, and dark blues. He had to get over . . . and now.

He stood, wavering as he once again put weight onto his injured legs. He bent over and rubbed his thighs vigorously, trying, if not to warm them, then to at least hold the frostbite at bay. He looked around, ending with his head facing the starry sky. There was no choice. He would have to risk the wind and the cold. There was only one way across. With any luck, the guard on the other side would also be facing away from the line and toward the island. And with even more luck, Challies's arms and legs would not fail him.

Still panting from the effort and adrenaline, Challies turned back toward the island, strode with trembling legs to where his Stær gun had fallen, and picked it up. As he lifted it to his holster, he saw the green light flash, as if there were a loose electrical connection somewhere in the gun.

"Not now," he muttered to himself. He tapped the gun with his left hand, and the light glowed without a flicker. He shook it just to make sure. Green. Satisfied, he holstered the weapon and stepped back up to the Zipp line.

NINE

"WON'T BE LONG NOW!" TOM SHOUTED over the din of the aircraft's engines. Máire nodded but didn't look at him. White-knuckled, she gripped her chest straps and stared straight ahead. She tried to ignore the thin film of sweat that covered her face and neck, as well as the drops that worked their way down the small of her back. With every lurch of the plane, she gasped and then clenched her teeth to hide her fear.

To her left, the heavily armed spotters chatted among themselves. Some laughed, some gesticulated as they spoke, but they all seemed relaxed. Máire knew that none of them had ever flown before, yet somehow they all acted as though flying were a daily occurrence . . . no more extraordinary than brushing their teeth. Seeing them reminded her of the ACF Protectors she'd known back in Ætheria. Unlike the Cthonian spotters, the only weapons the Ætherians really possessed were Stær guns. These weren't fatal, but they did make an impressive flash when fired, and the person struck by one of their projectiles would be instantly incapacitated, their body pumped with one hundred thousand volts. She wondered how dangerous the Cthonians' weapons were. She'd seen them when she'd first arrived, and she'd seen them here and there back in the Cave Complex. But looking at the rifles now she realized she'd never seen one fired. Were they lethal? Or did they just stun?

Just as she did when she lived in Ætheria, Máire hated weapons of any sort.

Tom leaned over and nudged her elbow. She

tilted her head to listen, but kept her eyes focused straight ahead.

"If it's okay with you, I'd like to go over the plan again," he shouted.

"Okay. Go ahead," she said at a normal volume. As soon as she spoke, she wondered if he'd heard her.

"We're going to land about a hundred yards or so from the impact site and where the explosion occurred. The first people out will be the spotters. They're going to secure the area. Their orders are to scour the site for any hostiles, and then to set up defensive positions around the perimeter. Half of them will form a human shield. They'll protect us. The other half's assignment is to begin excavating for remains . . . for our team that died, that is. Who knows if there are any Ætherians in there?" He shrugged. "While they do that, I'll go with you to search the rubble. Your goal is to see if you can get any clues from the Ætherian remains to help us make sense of what they may be up to up there."

"What will they do if they find anyone . . . any . . . bodies?"

"There," Tom shouted, pointing towards the front of the plane. Strapped to the wall separating the cargo area from the cockpit were the three containers she'd seen earlier. Each was the size of a small sofa. "Those contain forensic kits. Body bags. Gloves. Hazmat suits. That kind of thing. If they find anyone, we'll have to bring them back to the CCC. There, we can proceed to identification, recognition, and burial. We'll see."

"And what if I find . . . something?" she asked. She looked at him for the first time since taking off. Her eyes were wide and glossy.

Tom cleared his throat. "Well, we'll log it and, if need be, take it back. We'll also need you to tell me what you think each, um, item is before moving on. Remember: you're our detective here. Our sleuth, so to speak."

Máire lowered her head, lost in thought. With a

whine, the airship's engines suddenly slowed. Her stomach lurched as she felt the machine dip.

"What's that?" she snapped, looking around with panicked eyes. "What's happening?"

"Nothing! Try to relax! We can't fly too high because of the cloud—we don't know what would happen if we were to fly up into it. As it is, the engineers are already nervous enough about these machines' reliability. But that's why the airship bounces around like that." He looked at his watch. "Besides, I also think we're landing, that's all. We should be on the ground in just a few minutes."

———

"Landing zone in sight. All clear. No sign of hostile elements," the pilot's crackling voice boomed through a small black speaker attached to the front cargo wall. "Prepare for landing."

The airship shuddered as it slowed from forward thrust to a hover. The nose tilted upward and the roar of the engines became deafening. Máire couldn't see through the small windows opposite her, but she imagined that the turbines must be rotating so that their wash was pointing downward. She clutched the shoulder straps so tightly the canvas bit into her palms.

The spotters grew quiet as the airship lowered. With a jolt, the wheels touched down and the engines slowed, allowing the machine to come to a full rest. Almost instantly, the whir and whine that had become so mind-numbing faded as the power to the turbines was cut.

Several dozen metallic clicks echoed through the cargo hold. Acting as one, the spotters unbuckled their straps and stood.

"It's time," Tom said. "We're here."

Máire turned to her left and gave a start. Tom was already unbuckled and standing. But she had been so wrapped up in her fear of flying that she didn't even notice. With the airship grounded, she felt a wave of relief. And with jelly-like fingers, she unlatched herself and stood.

"Wait," Tom said, holding up a hand.

"What is it?" Máire asked.

"Standard procedure. Even though the scanners and the pilot don't see anything, the spotters still have to secure the area. So we wait here until we get the signal."

"How long will that take?"

"Just a few minutes."

The plane's rear ramp opened, and the spotters poured out. They were more tense than before. Their rifles were lowered and pointed outside. When their feet touched the Cthonian soil, they fanned out in all directions. From her position deep in the airship, Máire had the impression they were moving in a specific formation. Some rushed toward the front of the plane, some ran at a right angle to the fuselage, and some ran straight back. But all swept their weapons side to side as they marched, ready for any surprise.

After a few tense minutes of waiting and wondering with Tom, Máire jumped when one of the spotters suddenly reappeared in the plane's open hatch.

"Sir! All clear!" The soldier paused, his eyes on Tom. Máire noticed the man's name tag read Hector.

"Good work," Tom answered. "You know what to do."

"Yes, sir. The others are already taking up positions."

"Tell the forensics team they can come back and get their things. Let's do this."

"Done!" Hector disappeared. Shouted orders echoed out somewhere behind the plane.

"You ready?" Tom asked, turning to Máire.

She nodded and swallowed.

"Okay, let's go."

The two walked toward the back of the airship and climbed down the ramp. Even though the early hints of dawn were still nothing more than a faint, greenish glow, Máire's eyes had grown accustomed to the airship's darkness. She squinted against the new, dim light. As her eyes adjusted, she took in a panorama that she'd last seen sixteen years before.

As she remembered, all around was flat sand, stretching in all directions. Turning around and glancing at the front of the plane, she realized she was facing west. The aircraft must've made a U-turn midair to land facing the Cthonian complex. Perhaps to make taking off easier to get home? But from here, the cave was completely invisible. It was blocked both by several hundred miles and a dark blue mountain range stretching up from the horizon. She turned back around to face the plane's rear.

About a hundred yards off to her left, the body of the other airship lay inert, like some giant beached whale. The painted exterior was marred by hundreds of dings and scratches, some the size of an entire person. As she stepped away from her plane, the pre-dawn light played off of the surface of the damaged vehicle, showing that it was covered in dents and gashes. The airship looked as though it had been in an accident, but one that had left mostly superficial damage—nothing structural.

To know what kind of accident, all she had to do was turn her eyes to the plane's right. There, erupting from the sand like a volcano range, the massive mound of a building's rubble rose toward the sky. The pile was thin at the ends, but grew thicker toward the middle, reaching what must've been thirty or forty feet into the air. The whole mass was about thirty or forty yards long, but from her vantage point, she couldn't tell how wide it was. She paused, allowing her eyes to absorb the scene of destruction.

Hundreds of wires, metal struts, turf, I beams, glass, fiberglass, cloth, concrete, white shreds of canvas, rope, and even clumps of dirt tumbled and crumbled together, writhed and twisted in a chaotic blend of human engineering . . . that had crashed from the sky and obliterated everything that had been achieved over the past several hundred years.

Somewhere underneath the mound, Cthonia's own water emissary force lay crushed, devastated by the force of tons of man-made structure falling from thirty thousand feet. *Had they felt anything?* she wondered. *Or had it been instant? A crash and then dark? And the people in Tátea Power Works at the time of the crash? The fall from the stratosphere must've lasted at least a few minutes—a long time to think about what was about to happen.*

Black, acrid coils of smoke bled from several dozen spots on the pile, like water oozing from a sponge. Máire couldn't see any flames. They must've been buried deep in the simmering debris. Because the wind was blowing from west to east, the smoke was being lifted and carried away from her. The only smell that greeted her nostrils was one she'd smelled many times before: the sandy wasteland that was Cthonia.

This was part of the world she'd known for most of her life. A world that now seemed to be crumbling as she watched.

And her son?

Just beyond the smoking debris, a massive crater marred the earth. Spanning nearly fifty feet, the hole had clearly been made by a violent explosion. Frozen geysers of rock and dust extended across the sand in all directions, having been blown away by an erupting ball of fire. Here and there, chunks of reddish piping lay about, torn and broken, resembling severed pieces of an airship's fuselage. Some pieces were flattened, some held their shape, some were little more than shreds of metal. Máire looked directly up from the crater, her gaze stretching up to the clouds and then back down to the rubble. She realized that she was looking at remains of the Proboscis, Ætheria's only lifeline.

What she didn't know was that she was also seeing the remains of a massive explosion of underground cthoneum gas, ignited by Brondl's hasty attack on the Proboscis.

Beyond the Proboscis's remains, starting hundreds of yards in the north and stretching miles off to the east, hundreds, if not thousands, of taut guy wires and vertical metal struts stretched from concrete foundations planted in the Cthonian sand, where they disappeared into the roiling yellowish Welcans cloud far above. At regular one- or two-hundred-yard intervals, the guy wires emerged from the cloud in an irregular oval shape and stretched out to burrow into the ground, forming a much larger but identical shape. Máire knew that these particular wires anchored individual islands. Because they narrowed as they rose, they formed arrows pointing out each installation of the Ætherian settlement. As she traced the islands' wire silhouettes with her eyes, she tried to imagine the archipelago as she remembered it.

The only other feature of this scene of devastation was the remains of Cthonian mining and water extraction machines that slumbered off to the right, about sixty yards from where the Proboscis had been. Next to a piece of machinery that looked like a tractor attached to a thirty-foot-tall drill bit, several triangular piles of soil served as a testament to the spotters' work progress in searching for ground water. *If only they hadn't attacked,* Máire thought, scanning the remains, *maybe they would've found some. But now what? No water, and so much death . . .*

Máire's eyes fell back onto the smoldering rubble, which lay about fifty yards away. She scanned the whole scene again, which was becoming more and more visible as the darkness faded into an eerie, greenish light. By now the spotters had fanned out around the site, their weapons drawn. The other team of forensics were setting up to the left of the pile. They had planted their containers in the sand and were opening them and pulling out the contents. As some of the spotters donned gloves and protective masks, others chatted and pointed to different spots in the remains.

"How are we going to do this?" Máire asked.

"We need to be careful," Tom answered. "We haven't had a chance to explore this place. And this is being considered both a crime scene and a hazard. We can't just climb all over. Because we might contaminate evidence or cause a collapse. We've already lost enough people here. We don't need any more accidents." Tom began walking toward the "crime scene" as he spoke. Máire kept pace at his side.

"You and I will start by working our way around the perimeter. We'll go slowly. All we need from you right now is to scan every square inch of this mess that you can see, without climbing in. If you see anything that might be important, let me know."

"What about the others?" she asked.

"The forensics folks," he pointed, "are going to look for bodies. We'll start right there and move counterclockwise, away from them. Sound okay?"

Máire nodded. The two approached the rubble.

And then the wind shifted. Announced first by the tendrils of smoke that wafted in their direction, the breeze swirled and picked up, now lumbering from east to west . . . over the wreckage and straight toward Máire and Tom.

Máire gagged and threw her hands to her face. Tom also covered his mouth and nose. In all her life, Máire had never smelled anything so putrid. It was a mixture of burnt wood, melted metal, sizzling plastic, and rotting meat. She imagined it must be the smell of dead bodies.

As the stench enveloped her, numbers flashed through Máire's mind. How many people had been on Tátea when its Power Works had collapsed? She remembered hearing once that several hundred people were required to keep Ætheria's water, cthoneum processing, and electricity running. But did that mean that they had all been on the island at the time of the plant's destruction? Or had there been fewer? Or more? And in the Cthonian command post tents? Forty spotters had been there when the explosion and collision had occurred. So that meant that there could be several hundred bodies buried before her eyes. Buried, burning, or rotting.

"Sorry about that," Tom blurted out through

his fingers. "I didn't think to tell you that we might encounter . . . um . . . *that*. Part of the job, I guess."

"Can we move farther to the other side first?" she asked, lifting her chin to point.

"What do you mean?"

"Around the other side, the wind will be coming against us from the desert. Not from that."

Tom shrugged his shoulders.

"I don't see why not."

This time Máire took the lead.

When they had reached a point where the wind covered them with a refreshing draft, Máire eased her hands away from her face and took a few tentative breaths. Smelling only the arid Cthonian air, she relaxed and lowered her arms. She took a deep breath to cleanse her lungs, held it for a few seconds, and released. She stepped closer to the rubble.

Because the Ætherian building had flattened out when it had landed, she could approach the pile by navigating her feet between the tangle of wires, bent poles, and shredded tecton. With each step, she made sure to place her feet squarely on sand and not to bump into any of the "evidence," as Tom had called it. He stuck close to her, but she ignored his presence. Instead, she bit her lip to hold her emotions at bay while she allowed her eyes to scan the wreckage.

At first, it was difficult to spot anything recognizable . . . almost like staring into the nighttime sky and noticing constellations only after gazing for several minutes. Here, too, objects began to emerge from the chaos: she saw tattered bits of turf—the same turf she'd walked on *before*; she saw the smooth building materials that had formed Ætheria's Power Works exterior; she saw shattered remains of the transit tubes that snaked over most of Ætheria's islands; she saw what could only have been the sheetrock forming the Power Works' interior walls; she saw wires; she saw water pipes, some still dripping with the remains of purified water; she saw burned bits of cloth; and, mixed in with the rubble, she saw shreds of white tecton that she knew had formed the Cthonian command post that had been obliterated in the disaster. As she noticed the individual items from her former world, she pointed them out to Tom and explained what they were. She also described what she could remember of Ætheria's layout, indicating how each piece fit into the bigger puzzle of the Ætherian archipelago.

She continued her counterclockwise walk around the destruction.

"Look," she said, stopping.

"Something else?"

"Yes. See that?" She pointed to the remains of the Proboscis. Tom nodded.

"Um-hm."

"That's part of the Proboscis."

"Proboscis?"

"That's what we called the pipe that came down to the ground here. It pulled up water and natural gas. You know, it's the thing the command group blew up."

"Oh. Yes. Right." Tom seemed embarrassed.

He straightened up. "Why did they call it the 'Proboscis'?"

Máire shrugged. "What somebody told me once was that when they built Ætheria and figured out this system, they named it after the part of a mosquito."

"What do you mean?"

"Well, mosquitos used to be much more common than they are now, what with all the dryness on Cthonia. They live on animals' and people's blood. They stick in a part on their nose that works like a needle and just suck. That's what a proboscis is."

"So, like a parasite?"

"Yes."

"Hmm." Tom narrowed his eyes in thought.

"The problem now is," Máire continued, "that by cutting that, we've basically cut Ætheria's water and electricity. I know they have some oxygen and water stores up there, but I don't know how long they'll last. As for the oxygen, most people don't get to use it, even though the air is dangerously thin up there."

Máire shook her head subtly.

"Yes, so now they're in the same boat as us," she said. "Neither the Cthonians nor the Ætherians have water. I'm worrying that both sides are getting desperate. I know how long *we* can last with our reserves. What I don't know is how long they can last . . . nor how worried they might be. But . . . given that . . . given what I know about their Head Ductor, they're probably pretty anxious right now." Her eyes glazed over as her thoughts drifted to the wreckage of her past.

Without waiting for Tom's cue, she continued her walk. Tom followed.

After twenty or thirty minutes or more of the same, Tom stopped suddenly.

"Oh, look!"

Máire turned and followed Tom's gaze.

There, about ten feet up from the ground, a hand jutted out from the side of the rubble. One glance revealed immediately that they were looking at an Ætherian hand; a still intact Tracker was fastened to the wrist. The hand was desiccated. Its skin had drawn in on the bone like some sort of rubber puppet hand with all the air sucked out. The flesh was grossly discolored. The Ætherians were already naturally much darker than the pale Cthonians, but this hand seemed almost black.

At the sight of the hand, Máire felt a wave of terror. She knew that every Tracker bore the name and identity code of its wearer, and that only members of the Ætherian Cover Force, the High Command, and the Ætherian Council wore them. She knew that at sixteen, Rex was too young to be a part of the ACF, but perhaps the Tracker belonged to someone else she knew. Perhaps . . .

"I have to see who that is," she said in a trembling voice.

"What do you mean?"

"That person was a member of the Ætherian

Cover Force. It's like the Ætherian army and police combined, but mostly for patrolling . . . "

Without waiting for the all-clear from Tom, she began scrambling up the side of the mound. Pieces of debris shifted and crunched under her weight. She gritted her teeth and plowed forward, gripping onto whatever she could use as a handhold: plastic, stratoneum, turf, pipes . . . "Hey!" Tom shouted, lunging after her. "We're not authorized to do that! Only the forensics team can . . . "

Before he'd finished his sentence, she'd already stopped climbing and stood upright, panting. Several strands of hair fell in front of her sweat-covered face. Her eyes were fixed on the hand, which was now just a yard from her feet.

"Edgar," she said.

"What's that?" Tom huffed behind her.

"This person's name was Edgar." She shook her head. "No idea who that is."

"Okay then. Let's keep moving. And no more climbing into that rubble. If you get injured or destroy some evidence, I'll have to account for it. This is just too important to be mucking around."

Máire eased her way down to solid ground.

The morning grew warmer as the two made it around the pile of debris to where they once again could see the two airships. When the damaged airship came into view, Máire noticed a small swarm of spotters walking in and out of its cargo hold, while others seemed to be inspecting the outside. A few of the spotters pointed to different parts of the dented fuselage and chatted with each other, shaking their heads. Far off to her left, the forensics team was busy at work. She gave a start; several six-foot-long plastic bags lay on the ground in a neat row.

Bodies.

"Who are they?" she asked, fear staining her voice. "In the bags."

"Them?" Tom answered. "Hang on." He pulled his radio receiver from his belt and pressed the transmit button. There was a click of static, and Tom spoke into the device.

"Forensics, this is Caput Brun."

One of the forensics team paused in his work and looked over at Tom and Máire. He pulled his own radio from his belt and raised it to his head. Seconds later, Tom's receiver hissed a reply.

"This is forensics, what's up?" The spotter waved as he spoke. Máire shook her head. She thought it was a little silly to be radioing to each other, when a shout would do. The team was only thirty or forty yards away, after all.

"Do you have an ID on the bodies?" Tom asked.

"Yes. All our own. We also found a skull, but no skeleton. Everything's pretty badly burnt up."

Tom shot a glance at Máire. His brow creased in a worried look. "You mean the bodies are all Cthonians? From the command post?"

"That's right. We're going to keep looking."

"Thanks."

Tom looked at Máire and shrugged his shoulders. "Well, there you go."

The two continued their search. But they had not

taken ten steps before Tom grabbed Máire's arm, halting her. His sudden movement made her jump.

"There's another one!" he said, pointing to a spot thirty feet away at the foot of the debris pile.

A surge of fear filled Máire. She looked around frantically, trying to spot what Tom had seen. But all she saw was more rubble.

"Where?!" she snapped.

"There! On the ground! It's one of those things!" Without waiting for her to answer, Tom bolted ahead in a run. He'd covered several dozen feet and slowed, leaning over. He scooped something out of the sand. He turned back and walked toward Máire, his eyes fixed on whatever he held in his hands. With one hand, he clutched his find. With the other, he dusted it off. His face revealed curiosity mixed with the satisfaction of having found something important.

"What is it?" Máire asked as Tom neared.

He looked up and held out his hand. "Look."

There, like a black circle in the middle of his pale

Cthonian palm, lay an Ætherian Tracker. Separated from its bearer. But it was intact. A wave of thoughts overwhelmed Máire's mind. Whose was it? What had happened? If the Tracker was intact but not on its bearer's arm, that meant that something must've happened to separate the person's arm from the device. A severed hand or arm, for example . . . these were the only things Máire could think of that would allow the Tracker to slip off. But who? How? Whose name was on it?

As her worries gained in intensity she lunged forward and snatched the Tracker from Tom's open hand. He flinched at her sudden movement, but checked himself before shouting, "Hey!" He knew she still had her son and probably friends in Ætheria, and that she'd moved only because she needed to know. She needed closure.

As if afraid for Tom to see her reaction, Máire turned her back on him to look at the Tracker. With heart pounding in her ears, she eased her fist open to reveal the shiny black circle within. Her first thought was wonder; how had it emerged from the cataclysm with not so much as a scratch? The surface was as smooth and pristine as when the Tracker had first been manufactured. But what had happened to the bearer?

She closed her eyes slowly. She took a deep breath, gaining the courage to go through with it. She turned the Tracker over to reveal its wider side . . . the side on which the bearer's name was engraved.

From where he stood, Tom could see Máire's dark Ætherian skin go pale as the blood left her face. Her legs seemed to falter. One arm reached out and snatched at the air. She seemed to be grasping for something to hold on to . . . something to keep from falling. She gasped for breath. She opened and closed her mouth a few times as if to speak, but nothing came out.

"Are you okay?" Tom said, stepping forward. He rushed to her side and grabbed her hand. She instantly leaned into his arm. He worried that if he didn't hold her up, she might faint. He reached around her back and squeezed her torso, lifting her up.

She gulped. She mouthed mute words. She closed her eyes. And then, without warning . . .

"NOOOO!" she screamed, pushing Tom off with an astounding, almost superhuman strength. Tom stumbled to her side and caught his balance, standing. The spotters around them spun in their direction, their rifles trained and ready for any sign of a hostile enemy. But they saw none. All they saw was a pale Ætherian woman giving way to despair.

"NOOOO!" she screamed again. Her strained, horrified voice echoed off of the desert's emptiness. In the next breath, she hurled the Tracker away from her and toward the rubble, where it disappeared with a clank. "Why? Is he . . . can he . . . noooooo!"

"What is it!?" Tom roared. "Talk to me, now!"

"My son!" she wailed. "This belonged to Franklin—his foster father! If Franklin's dead, what happened to him . . . to my Rex!" And no sooner had she uttered her son's name than she hurled herself onto the pile of smoldering debris, throwing bits and pieces of her destroyed former life behind her as she frantically searched for her son's body.

"Máire, stop!" Tom shouted. He dropped his rifle, lunged forward, and grabbed Máire by the waist, hurling her away from the wreckage with all his strength. She let out a pained groan and tumbled backward onto the ground. As she landed on her back, her head rapped against the sand. Tom immediately regretted pulling her so hard. He hadn't meant to hurt her, only get her out of the dangerous rubble.

If she was hurt, she didn't show it. No sooner had she landed in the dust than she sprang back up, her eyes wild and fixed on the spot where he'd found the Tracker. She sprang forward, but Tom planted both hands on her shoulders and squeezed.

"Stop it!" he screamed, his face just inches from hers. "Listen to me!" By this time, several of the spotters had wandered over. Their facial expressions revealed their confusion. Should they restrain her? Just wait for an order? In their uncertainty, they formed a semicircle around the two, their rifle muzzles dangling aimlessly toward the ground.

"What's wrong?" Tom snapped, his eyes glaring. "Talk to me!"

"That belonged to the man who was taking care of my son." She motioned with her head in the direction she'd dropped the Tracker. "The only way it could come off is if he's dead!"

"How do you know it was his?"

"His name was on it! And the HD told me where Rex would go!"

"But it's not your *son's* Tracker. Isn't that all that matters?"

"It . . . but . . . " she stammered, her eyes rolling towards his. "Wha . . . ?"

"If this guy is dead, how does that mean anything about your son?"

Máire hesitated, her thoughts churning.

"He worked there. In the Power Works," she mumbled, more to herself than to Tom. "And there the building is."

"Well," Tom released her shoulders and stood tall. "The only way Rex could even be in all this is if he were in the Power Works when it fell. Right?"

The glint in Máire's eyes shifted from panic to relief. Her muscles relaxed. As she realized that her panic had been unfounded, she slowly nodded her head.

"You're right. Let's get back to it."

But just as they turned to continue their search, someone screamed from the direction of the damaged airship.

TEN

THE WIND HOWLED IN CHALLIES'S EARS AS HE stepped onto the Zipp line platform. The gusts pushed his body, causing him to grip the stratoneum handrails leading up to the takeoff podium. Part of him felt drawn to look over the edge of the island and into the dark void, but he knew he needed to stay focused on his goal. His arms and legs were already trembling enough, and his thighs had become numb from the pain. But right now, he couldn't afford to lose his grip on the wire.

The wire. Every island in the Ætherian archipelago was connected to at least one other via several razor-tight, half-inch-thick braided wires, each two yards apart. These Zipp lines had always been intended to be used with high-grade pulleys and state-of-the-art harnesses. In the history of the stratospheric complex, no one had ever attempted to cross one by hand or unharnessed. To do so was unheard of, unthinkable even. If the sixty-mile-per-hour winds did not push you off, the frigid wire would certainly cause you to lose feeling in your hands. Either way, the result was death.

Challies knew all of this.

But still, he had no choice.

With his eyes locked on the wire that stretched off into the night, he reached down and pulled each of his gloves tight. He glanced at his holstered Stær gun. The green light no longer flickered. It shone steadily, indicating the weapon's readiness to fire.

He took a deep breath and closed his eyes. He took another, this time focusing on calming his nerves. He turned around so that his back was facing the platform's edge. He knew it would be better to back his way across the gap. That would make pulling himself across easier. He wouldn't have to flounder in an awkward shuffle forward.

Or so he thought.

Challies opened his eyes, looked up, and stretched for the wire with both hands. He felt the tight new AG suit pull against his arms, legs, and joints. He had to stand on his toes to reach it. With a grunt and a lunge, he closed his fingers around it and tightened his abdominal muscles, pulling his wounded legs up. He hooked his left leg over the wire, allowing it to settle into the back of his knee. He did the same with his right leg. He pulled his lower legs downward, forming an inverted V with both legs. He locked his inner elbows over the wire, so that he felt hooked in with his stronger muscles. For he knew that his hands would tire much too quickly.

He began to shuffle across.

Inch by inch, Challies quickly developed a rhythm: slide his knees forward until they almost touched his elbows, and then work his elbows up until his back flattened out. Repeat. In his movement, he resembled an upside-down caterpillar. As he eased his way out, he kept his eyes skyward, where they focused on one star that shone brighter than the others. The star became his beacon and anchor. It helped him to control his breathing and his fear. Because he was so high up in the atmosphere, it didn't twinkle . . . nor did any of the others. It was like staring into a sea of lights.

The moment Challies cleared the platform and left the safety net of the Sanatorium Complex behind, he was hit by a blast of freezing air from below. Because he was no longer protected by the massive man-made structure, he was open to the elements. His body swayed in the wind. With each gust, a new shot of adrenaline surged through his body, causing his panic to rage, but at the same time his arms and legs felt no pain or effort. At this point, he'd almost forgotten about his torn legs. At the first blast of wind, he paused, waiting for it to pass. But it soon became clear that to cross the Zipp line unaided was to be battered like a wind sock. He shook his head and continued.

Inch by inch.

As he neared the middle of the line, he wondered—if only for a brief instant—how he could detect no dip in the wire and no slack. He'd never learned how the wires had been first installed, but whoever had done it had done an excellent job of pulling them iron-rod tight. They felt more like solid poles than woven wires. In his life—and especially since he'd joined the ACF—he'd crossed the Zipp lines hundreds, if not thousands, of times. But he'd never paid attention to the devices' mechanics. He'd only harnessed himself in and zipped across, like everyone else in Ætheria.

Challies kept his eye on the star and slid his now-cramping arms and legs over the wire. He had no idea how long he'd been dangling and swinging there in the wind, but his muscles had begun to sting and tremble from the effort. How far across was he? He tilted his head back and looked, upside-down, towards Island Twenty-Three, where he was headed.

He froze. The island's edge loomed twenty feet away, its Zipp line platform beckoning in the starlight. Just beyond the platform, Challies made out the grayish silhouette of an ACF guard. Just like the other, he was standing with his legs shoulder-width apart and arms behind his back. *Were they ordered to stand this way?* Challies thought. Like the other guard, this one was also facing the island . . . not the chasm between them.

It was just as Challies had hoped.

Seeing the guard sent a wave of renewed, adrenaline-fueled energy into his aching limbs. He stopped. The wind howled around him, sending him bouncing up and down. He grimaced at the pain in his elbows and knees. But now wasn't the time to let that overcome him. He'd made it this far. With the rush of energy came a rush of hope—for the first time since he'd watched Aral and Rex flee over the Zipp line with the pulleys, he felt that he actually had a chance to escape . . . alive. He could do this. He had to.

Challies took a deep breath and worked his right arm off of the wire. He now hung by his knees and left elbow. The wind never let up and threatened to toss him off like a rag doll at any second. He clenched his teeth and reached down with his right hand, feeling his way to his utility belt and his Stær gun. He unholstered the weapon, his hand clutching the grip and his index finger easing its way to the trigger. He rose the gun in front of him and aimed.

At that moment, the wind shifted direction. It no longer swept up from below but slammed into his left side. Was it because he was near the island? Was the island pushing the wind around in violent eddies? He hesitated, waiting for the gale to steady. A minute passed. The wind seemed settled in its left-to-right course. Challies knew that if he aimed directly at the guard, this wind would push the Stær projectiles off to the right. He'd likely miss. And then what? The guard would immediately hear him, and that would be it.

He shifted his aim. He cleared his mind of all thoughts. He let out a breath halfway.

And pulled the trigger.

Pop-thwoomp!

The Stær gun fired, emitting a blinding burst of sparks into the night. Challies blinked. There was a *swoosh* and a thump somewhere up ahead in the dark. After that, no sounds. Just the wind and Challies's pounding heart. He blinked again, trying to force his night vision back.

And then he saw it. There, in the middle the Zipp line platform, the guard's inert body lay in a heap. Challies's shot had hit its target.

In a rush of exhilaration, Challies hurried along the final twenty feet of the line with both hands and legs. When he sensed the platform below him, he released his grip. He fell with a bony clump, his body coming to rest next to the guard's on the stratoneum landing platform.

For several minutes, Challies didn't move. Bit by bit, he worked his arms and legs, massaging them and stretching them, trying to chase the pain away. In addition to the searing pain of the lacerations on his thighs, it felt as though his elbows and knees had been crushed in a vice. He soon worried that he'd harmed his joints too much to continue. As the adrenaline rush faded, the pain grew. Had he broken his arms? Torn his ligaments? Ripped a muscle? He continued to work his smarting limbs, letting his head roll to the left as he did.

With the sound of the wind, he couldn't hear the guard's breathing. He knew that Stær gun blasts were not lethal . . . typically. The guard would wake up soon. And in the case of this one, he would have no memory of what happened. After all, he hadn't seen Challies sneak up—just like Roman back in the Sanatorium. So much the better.

Challies tried to sit up. He eased his sore arms to the platform and pushed himself up. To his surprise, his muscles worked once more and, though prickling with pins and needles, showed no sign of injury. He grimaced as he shook them awake, but he felt reassured that he could continue. He worked himself to a standing position.

Now that his night vision was returning, he glanced around before moving. It was Island Twenty-Three, where the descent pod hangar was located. Not wanting to risk breaking through a Larder trap door again and not knowing how to open the hatches, his only chance was make his way into the building and escape down the same way as Aral and Rex.

Challies looked around to convince himself he hadn't been seen. Satisfied that he was alone, he slid up to the inert guard and ran his hands over the man's waist, searching. His fingers clasped around a flat plastic card attached the man's belt by an elastic lanyard. It was his Nanokepp Card. This time he didn't forget. Without hesitating, Challies snapped the card away and stood. He turned towards the warehouse door and staggered the remaining yards between him and his way out of Ætheria.

"God, please work, please work," he muttered to himself as he lifted the card to the magnetic sensor to the right of the door frame. If this ACF guard had been stationed to watch the Zipp platform on Island Twenty-Three, one of the archipelago's most secure islands, then surely his Nanokepp Card would open . . .

"Hey!"

A voice screaming over the wind caused Challies to whip around and face the Zipp platform. In his alarm, he dropped the card and instinctively drew his Stær gun. And no sooner had it fallen from his grip than the ever-present jet stream snatched it away, sending it fluttering end-over-end over the island's edge. It was gone.

Challies had no time to process his loss before he saw where the shout had come from. He had expected it to be the dazed guard who had woken up, but was horrified when he saw a team of five

ACF Protectors zipping across the expanse he'd just crossed by hand. Their headlamps glaring through the night like enraged demons' eyes, they had slid out onto the Zipp line together, forming a spectacle Challies had never seen before. In all his years in Ætheria, and even since he'd become an ACF Protector, he'd only ever known one person at a time to cross the expanses between islands.

"You there!"

"Stop!"

"Don't move!"

"Drop the weapon!"

"Make the right choice!"

His thoughts clouded by panic, Challies stepped toward the Zipp line platform, where the dazed ACF guard still lay unconscious. He raised his Stær gun with unsteady hands and aimed at the first Protector in the line, who was about thirty yards away.

Thwoomp-crack!

A burst of sparks belched from the weapon's

muzzle, blinding Challies and illuminating the Protectors' surprised faces in a flash. But instead of the projectile's shooting straight ahead, the gun jerked violently in Challies's hand, and a divot flew from the turf fifteen feet in front of him. A weak sizzle of sparks darted out from the impact site like tiny lightning bolts.

Challies had missed.

"Freeze!" the first Protector shouted into the night as he planted his feet on the landing platform. As he unhooked his harness, he cast a glance at his comrade's inert body but quickly leapt from the landing platform and shot back. Two of the others fired as well, before they had even reached the island. A dazzling show of sparks created an orangish strobe effect on the south side of the warehouse, while the screaming wind blew the Stær charges into the air like fireworks. The five ACF shouted at once, but Challies couldn't make out their jumbled words—all he could tell was that they were furious and threatened. Like cornered wolves, they lunged forward onto the island, ready for a kill.

Challies knew he had no time to wait for his weapon's charge to reset. Swearing aloud, he hurled his Stær gun at the approaching Protectors in a desperate attempt to fight back. It flew through air and bounced off of the landing platform with a metallic *clunk*. He then turned and bolted alongside the building.

"Hey!" one of the Protectors screamed. Then, his chilling words made their way through the howling wind—words that Challies heard clearly. *Fsssclick.* "Fraser here, post 14-A. The suspect is in sight. We are in pursuit. I repeat, I have Challies 2496 in my sights and he is running northwesterly on Island Twenty-Three. He is rounding the parts warehouse now, but we've got him. There's nowhere he can go. Send backup *now!*" *Click.*

Ignoring the pain in his legs, Challies pumped his arms and ran. His breath came in short hisses. No thoughts clouded his mind—not even the reality that he was running into a trap. Like the other buildings in Ætheria, the warehouse was tear-drop-shaped and its turf-covered ground circled it like a track. All Challies could really hope to do was delay the inevitable. He ran counterclockwise, but the five ACF split into two groups: two men ran after him, while three ran clockwise, closing him into a pincer formation.

When Challies reached the western point of the building, a blast of northern wind pushed him two yards to the side, causing him to stumble. He fought to regain his balance. He leaned forward against the wind and pushed off with his battered legs again and again and again. He pushed and pumped until his legs burned even more and his lungs screamed from hypoxia. They ached, they labored, and they froze.

In the next second, the three ACF Protectors who had run to the right rounded the warehouse and sprinted straight for Ætheria's second-most-wanted fugitive. Challies had little time to react before they were upon him. The lead Protector pointed and shouted something to the others, who raised their Stær guns.

"Challies!" the lead Protector shouted. A wave of dread filled Challies. He recognized Roman's voice.

"Roman?" he cried back, coming to a halt. He struggled to stay upright against the throbbing, full-body pain of hypoxia. He wheezed but felt like he was getting no air. His head spun. His temples pounded. A scuffle behind him made him turn. The other two had rushed up behind him, their Stær guns pointed at him. He was surrounded.

"Challies!" Roman repeated, as if to convince himself that this was really his ACF partner. Roman took a few steps forward, lowering his unarmed hand and motioning for the others to wait. But Roman kept his gun drawn and trained on Challies.

"Roman?" Challies repeated.

"Challies, you have to stop. We know what you did. The Head Ductor knows."

"What are you going to do?" Challies's face

burned in embarrassment and anger the moment he'd spoken.

Roman paused. He seemed to be thinking of an answer. "That's not up to me. You know that! But there's nothing you can do now. Just come with us and be reasonable!"

Challies took several strained gulps of air. He swallowed heavily. He shook his head and stared straight at Roman's darkened face. "Reasonable? You know what will happen! I know. My brother Abel knows. He was Tossed—Tossed *without* a trial. For what? Giving oxygen out. To children! What do you *think* will happen to me?!"

Roman raised his hand as if to calm Challies. "No, no, no," he said. "You don't know that. How would . . ."

"I do know it!" Challies screamed. "How dare you say that! How dare you!"

Roman glanced at the others and then looked back at Challies. "You know that's not true. It's propaganda. Don't believe rumors. Here, you need to make the right decision . . . right now. Come on. Let's go without a fight. You know everyone gets a trial. You know that!"

Challies didn't answer right away. His shoulders heaved from the effort of his strained breathing. He looked once more at the Protectors behind him. Their Stær guns were still aimed straight at him, but they seemed to be keeping their distance. Challies wondered if they were following Roman's lead.

He turned back to his former partner, his head shaking. "They don't," he muttered.

"What?"

"They don't always have trials. Especially not when you act against the HD."

"But if you don't come now, whatever happens won't be good!"

Challies turned to the left and eyed the edge of island. Beyond the grayish, starlit turf, only darkness filled his field of vision. Darkness and far-off stars, which were indifferent to the injustices of Ætheria. Challies knew that with one jump from there all he had to do was relax and go to sleep. It could be his choice, not the Head Ductor's. Challies could take that power away from that cockroach.

"I can't do this," Challies mumbled, facing Roman once more. Then, with renewed energy, he shouted, "It's just too much! He's killing us! You know it!"

And with that, Challies exploded to the left, using his last energy in a final sprint to the edge of the island.

But he never made it to the edge.

In a blast of light and searing pain, one hundred thousand volts of electricity surged through his body, throwing him to the turf in an unconscious, writhing heap. All that remained now was to turn him over to the Head Ductor.

Only he would decide Challies's fate.

ELEVEN

A THUNDERING ROAR FROM OUTSIDE WOKE Aral and Rex.

"What's that?" Rex snapped, sitting up. For an instant, he glanced around in a panic, unsure of where he was. Then he remembered. The night before, he and Aral had hidden themselves in the below-floor cargo hold of the damaged Cthonian airship at the explosion site. Not long after they'd reached the airship and he'd lain down below deck, Aral had managed to locate the undamaged food and water stores from the destroyed Cthonian command post. After eating and drinking, Rex had fallen into a deep catatonic sleep. Now realizing where he was, he was at the same moment relieved to feel that his pounding headache from the night before had faded.

His relief was short-lived.

Next to him in the dark, Aral shuffled in place. Though he couldn't see her, he sensed her warmth and movement. He could also hear her breathing accelerate as the sound outside grew louder.

"It's an airship," she whispered.

Rex held his breath, listening. He soon recognized the sound he'd heard several days before, when his team had been attacked by air. He associated the sound with the pain of losing Yoné, the ACF scout who'd become a friend in their expeditions from Ætheria to Cthonia.

"Who do you think it is?" he asked. "The same people who came after us before?"

"I don't know. Don't move."

Rex felt his ears ring as the rumble outside became guttural, shaking the earth and causing the steel enclosing them to vibrate in its rivets. The roar soon blended into a whine, followed by a deafening rush of air and sand, as if the two were being buried alive by an impossibly large sandstorm. The screaming engines changed pitch and the sand outside whipped into a fury, shredding and scraping at the sides of their hideout's fuselage. Higher and higher and higher the turbines howled, before suddenly dropping in pitch and slowing. The power to the engines had been cut.

"They've landed," Aral said. "They're here. The Cthonians."

"What time is it?" Rex asked.

"I don't know. Hold on."

Afraid to make a noise, Aral inched up toward the trap door closing them in. With a soft grunt, she pushed upward against the door. It groaned and creaked on its hinges, and a sliver of blinding light appeared around the door's edge. It grew as Aral lifted. Squinting, Rex followed Aral's glowing silhouette. Like a spotter preparing for an ambush, she kept her eyes trained through the crack. She paused when the door had opened about six inches—high enough to be able to peer outside easily.

"What do you see?" Rex asked. At the sound of his voice, Aral lowered her right hand to silence him. She shook her head slightly.

"Right now, nothing. Just a bunch of clouds of dust. I think they landed that way." She lifted her hand from in front of Rex's face and pointed to the right. "That's where the sand's blowing from."

"What time do you think it is?"

"No idea. But we've slept well into the . . . Wait! Shh!" Aral eased the trap door shut with a click and crouched in the dark next to Rex.

"What?"

"Spotters," she whispered. "Lots of them. Cthonians. And they've got guns."

Rex couldn't see her, but he could tell her face was turned toward him. He thought he felt her hot breath against his sweaty forehead.

"Don't you want to talk to them? I don't know, surrender? Don't you think they'd help?"

Aral was quiet. Outside, Rex could hear some men shouting something to each other, but he couldn't make out the words. Their voices seemed to be coming from all directions. He felt surrounded.

"I . . . uh . . . it's just . . . " she stammered.

"Why don't we go out there? Talk to them? They'll see we're not armed! Don't you think . . . "

"Up in here!" a spotter's voice at the side door of the airship cut Rex's sentence short. Whoever it was, he was clearly standing at the threshold. "You four, over here!" he shouted again, this time with his head turned away from the metal interior. His voice echoed inside the plane's cargo hold.

"Yes, sir!" someone replied from farther away.

In the next second, a thunderstorm of heavy footsteps plodded through the airship as Cthonian spotters poured in. In the cargo hold, Rex and Aral breathed with their mouths open, trying not to make noise. Both kept their eyes riveted on the hold's trap door. Aral reached out in the dark to place her hand on Rex's shoulder. Finding it, she squeezed. *Don't move,* she thought, hoping that Rex would somehow sense her thoughts through her touch. *Stay still . . .*

"Any signs of activity?" the voice said, now directly above them.

"Nothing. How about the cockpit?"

"Do it."

More footsteps, sweeping toward the front of the plane.

"It's locked."

"Open it."

"Yes sir."

There was a pause, followed by several gut-wrenching, metallic thuds. It sounded as if someone was kicking the cockpit door, trying to force it open. With each kick, Aral and Rex's hide-out rattled and shook. Just inches above their heads, the trap door groaned in its frame as the spotter shifted his weight and stepped toward the cockpit. Another thud boomed from the front of the plane, this one stronger than the others.

"Got it!" someone said.

"Check it out," the man above them said.

Some rustling came from the front of the plane. Rex imagined a group of abnormally tall, pale, Cthonian spotters rummaging through the cockpit, though for what, he had no idea.

"Nothing, sir," the voice from the cockpit said.

"Let's do another sweep of the whole airship."

"Got it."

Aral's and Rex's breathing raced under the terror of listening to the search party pour through the airship, not knowing what they were looking for. The two were prepared to give themselves up, but they'd already been shot at once. In the dark hold, Rex turned his head toward Aral. Why wasn't she coming out? What was she waiting for? Did she know something that Rex didn't?

"Okay, let's head to the wreckage," the spotter

said after several interminable minutes of pounding and thumping throughout the fuselage. Without replying, the spotters vanished, their footsteps echoing in the direction of the door, where they disappeared two by two. Their voices continued to ricochet outside, but they seemed to be heading in a different direction.

When the Cthonians had gotten far enough away, Rex leaned toward Aral.

"Do you want to go out?"

"I'm really worried," she said. "I don't recognize any of those voices. I don't know what they're doing. Or what their orders are. And I don't know if they might be the same team that came after us before."

Rex felt his fear mixing with impatience. "So what? If we don't want to talk to them, how are we going to do this?"

"Wait, just wait. I need to think. Just let me make a plan."

Feeling his frustration mount, Rex stood and placed his hands on the trap door.

"Wait! What are you doing?" Aral snapped. Worry filled her voice. "They might see you!"

Rex paused, listening. The only sounds that either of them could hear was that of one or two voices in the distance. He could hear nothing else— no footsteps in the plane's main compartment, no shuffling outside the plane, no clanks or creaks that would reveal spotters' presence nearby.

"I just want to peek," Rex said, lifting. "One of us has to do something!"

The trap door was lighter than he expected. He pushed up with the top of his head and his hands, each planted to the side of his ears. The morning light crept in, stinging his retinas. From his position, he had a clear view through the airship's open door and outside. He squinted and watched.

About sixty yards away, the massive pile of rubble lay smoldering. Small wisps of smoke trickled upward here and there. At regular intervals around the wreckage, a Cthonian spotter stood, facing away from the debris. Each spotter clutched a rifle across their chest. They seemed to be expecting action. Farther to the left, a dozen or so spotters worked together, unarmed. They were pulling different tools from several large containers: plastic bags, masks, yard-long pliers, crowbars, and what looked like plastic overalls. They moved back and forth between the rubble and the boxes. Several spotters fanned out and poked around in the heap as if looking for something. But what? Rex wondered if they were looking for the remains of him and Aral. Did they think the two were dead? Were they trying to find the remains of their own command post team that was crushed in the Power Works' fall? That had to be it. Rex could think of no other solution.

"They're snooping around the crash site," he said to Aral. "I think they've forgotten about us . . . I mean, this plane, at least."

"Hmm," Aral said. "That makes sense. They must've gotten reinforcements or something and are doing their first look around. Investigating. That has to be it. When I was with them, I . . . "

"Wait," Rex interrupted.

"What?"

"There's a woman with them."

"But there are a lot of women that work as spotters. I was one of them, you know? Just I wasn't armed . . . "

"No, I mean, a *woman*. Someone who's not a soldier. And someone who . . . "

"What's she doing?"

"Hold on . . . "

Rex focused on the woman, who'd just appeared from the left side of the rubble. She was the only person he could see that wasn't dressed like the others—she was the only one who wasn't an armed spotter. She wore dark blue pants and a white, long-sleeved shirt. Her hair was pulled back into a tie behind her head. While the spotters either stood guard or explored the wreckage, she walked along almost leisurely, staring at the Power Works' remains with her hands behind her back. A male spotter walked along with her, nodding every now and then. She paused, said something to him, and pointed at something in the pile. He nodded and they continued.

But more than that, the woman was about a foot shorter than the others, and her skin was much darker . . . as if she'd grown up in an environment with much more exposure to ultraviolet light than Cthonians. She looked like . . . like an Ætherian.

Rex's blood froze.

Is that . . . ?

Aral wedged herself up beside Rex, pushing him aside several inches. She lifted her head next to his so that they could both see out.

"Ah . . . " She gasped. "That's her."

"Her?" Rex's breath failed him. He feared that the truth was staring him in the face, but he refused to believe it.

"Yes! Máire! That's her! The one in your picture! The one who always talked about you . . . about your . . . face. She's the Ætherian that's been living in Cthonia for the last sixteen years!"

Aral froze, her eyes engrossed on the woman. The woman rushed forward and snatched something small and black out of the spotter's hand. She turned the thing over in her hand, looking at it closely. And in the next second, she'd dropped it and was diving at the debris pile, screaming. She seemed like a person possessed. With frantic, uncontrolled movements, she dug at the rubble, throwing pieces behind her and yanking at wires, pipes, and struts that were much larger than she was and that were firmly wedged under tons of wreckage. She cried out, causing the other spotters to turn toward her in alarm; the one closest to her reached out and yanked her back. She tumbled onto the ground and bounded back up. But the spotter planted himself between her and the debris and held her in place with both hands. He was saying something to her, but neither Rex nor Aral could hear. Whatever he was saying seemed to have a calming effect on her.

Rex could clearly see her muscles relax and her head begin to nod.

He could wait no longer. He'd already waited sixteen years—that was long enough.

"Mom!" Rex screamed, throwing the trap door open with a clash. Several of the spotters outside whirled toward the airship in alarm.

"No!" Aral bellowed, scraping at Rex's leg, which was already disappearing through the top of the door. "Wait!"

Rex kicked back at her and she lost her grip. He pushed up with his arms and thrust his feet downward against the floor of the airship's main compartment. *Clang!* In the next fraction of a second, he was out the door and sprinting toward his mother.

"Mom!"

In her panicked search, Máire heard his voice and whirled around. Her face was pale and clammy, her hair was disheveled, and her shoulders heaved from the effort.

She gaped at the boy running across the sand . . . straight toward her. Confused, the spotters took several steps toward him but looked to Tom for direction. He shook his head in disbelief but held up his hand for them to stand back. He seemed as puzzled as they.

"Rex?" Máire's clear voice halted Rex as he ran. Gasping for breath, he stepped up to his mother, whose moistened eyes scanned his face. They rested on his left eye, which drooped from nerve damage at birth, and his mouth, whose left side was paralyzed, giving him a lopsided smile. For a moment, she seemed to be trying to convince herself that the boy she was seeing was actually the baby she'd left behind sixteen years before. Without a word, she stepped toward him, her arms outstretched.

"Mom?"

Before the two could reach each other, their path was cut short by a thundering explosion ten feet between them and the pile of rubble. With an ear-shattering *flam!*, bits of shattered stratoneum, shreds of tecton, and clods of dislodged Cthonian earth burst up from the ground in a six-foot-wide eruption that covered the two in dust. At the blast, Rex and Máire instinctively jumped aside, turning their faces away from the flying debris.

"Ah!" Rex cried, covering his eyes in horror. Máire let out a cry.

"What is that?!" Tom bellowed out behind her. He waved at two of the spotters closest to Rex. He pointed at the explosion site and snapped. "What is it?!"

The spotters bounded up and pushed Rex aside. Guns pointed downward, they stepped through the swirling dust, which was slowly wafting away to reveal the horror underneath.

There, twisted gruesomely at the center of the newly formed crater, a gelatinous body lay facedown in the dirt. It had fallen from above.

Rex took a step forward and peered through the cloud. From where he stood, he couldn't see the face, but he immediately saw that the person was short and dark. It was an Ætherian, and he was wearing the dark blue uniform of the ACF Rex instinctively looked at the person's wrist. There was no Tracker. But why?

Rex looked up at his mother, who stood agape on the other side of the still-warm corpse. Her eyes darted between the body, the spotters, the lingering dust, and the sky. She was pale from fright, but she seemed to be avoiding Rex's gaze.

One of the spotters took a step in and kneeled. He placed his hand on the body's shoulder and pulled. Rex felt his stomach turn as the body rolled over. Its bones had been pulverized from the fall and it folded over as if made of rubber.

With a sickening flopping sound, the body landed on its back. The momentum from the turn caused its head to loll in Rex's direction. The eyes, glazed and pale, rested on Rex's.

It was Challies. The only ACF Protector who'd helped him escape the Head Ductor's paranoia. And who was now dead.